Geronimo Stilton

THE DRAGON PROPHECY

THE FOURTH ADVENTURE
IN THE
KINGDOM OF FANTASY

Scholastic Inc.

New York   Toronto   London   Auckland
Sydney   Mexico City   New Delhi   Hong Kong

Library of Congress Cataloging-in-Publication data available.

ISBN 978-0-545-39351-5

Based on an original idea by Elisabetta Dami.

www.geronimostilton.com

Published by Scholastic Inc., 557 Broadway, New York, NY 10012. SCHOLASTIC and associated logos are trademarks and/or registered trademarks of Scholastic Inc.

Text by Geronimo Stilton
Original title *Quarto viaggio nel Regno della Fantasia*
Cover by Silvia Bigolin
Illustrations by Danilo Barozzi, Silvia Bigolin, and Giuseppe Giundani
Color by Christian Aliprandi
Graphics by Yuko Egusa and Marta Lorini

Special thanks to Kathryn Cristaldi
Translated by Julia Heim
Interior design by Kay Petronio

17 16 15 14 13   17 18 19 20 21/0

Printed in China   38

First printing, September 2012

Geronimo Stilton

I am a bestselling author and publisher of *The Rodent's Gazette*, the most famouse newspaper on Mouse Island. This is my fourth trip to the **KINGDOM OF FANTASY**.

Scribblehopper

I am Geronimo's official guide in the Kingdom of Fantasy. I'm not a published author, but I'm an amazing poet. My poems are the best, better than all the rest!

King Thunderhorn

I am the King of the Elves. I always appear as a white deer. My horns and hooves are made of pure gold.

Sterling

I am the Princess of the Silver Dragons. I'm not afraid to go into battle, and I know all the tricks to tame a dragon!

Sparkle

I am a silver dragoness. I work for Blossom, Queen of the Fairies, and love justice and all that is good.

Bitsy Luckybug

I am a tiny ladybug and the Princess of the Kingdom of Greenfields. I am small but do my best to help those in need!

Mixy von Troll

I am the cook for the trolls. I may look like a mess, but I am an amazing chef. Not that anyone appreciates me . . . especially that rotten Chief Horrid!

DON'T
EMBARRASS ME!

It was five o'clock on a Friday evening in autumn and I couldn't wait to leave the office. I was looking forward to a **peaceful** weekend at home *relaxing* in front of the fire with a good book. I could just picture myself in my favorite pawchair. . . .

Oh, excuse me. I haven't introduced myself!

My name is Stilton, *Geronimo Stilton*. I am the publisher of *The Rodent's Gazette*, the most famouse newspaper on Mouse Island.

Anyway, as I was saying, that evening I was about to turn off my computer and stop working when . . . the phone rang.

At that exact instant, my cell phone began playing my latest squeaktone. I had **THIRTY-FIVE text messages** in my in-box!

Then the fax machine started spitting out sheets of paper all over the room.

And the computer began shrieking like my Cheeseball the Clown alarm clock with the volume set on **Hysterical**.

BEEP BEEP BEEP BEEP BEEP BEEP BEEP!

I glanced at the screen. **Holey cheese!** I had received fifty-seven new emails!

What was going on?

I grabbed the phone, hoping to solve the mystery. **RATS!** It was my grandfather William Shortpaws. Nine times out of ten Grandfather calls only to **yell** at me.

This time he shouted, "Grandson, you better be ready for the grand opening! Don't **embarrass** me!"

Grand opening? I had no idea what Grandfather was talking about.

Then my cell phone rang again.

It was my sister, Thea. "**Hey, Gerry Berry!** Let me know if you need a photographer for the grand opening!" she squeaked before she hung up.

Grand opening? I had no idea what Thea was talking about.

I decided to go through my email. After all, I had **FIFTY-SEVEN MESSAGES**! The first was from my cousin Trap.

MESSAGE

From: Trap

Subject: BORING WEAR

Germeister,

Need something formal to wear to the grand opening. Can you lend me one of your stuffy suits?

Trap

I scratched my head.

Grand opening? I had no idea what Trap was talking about.

I started to read my text messages, but I didn't get past the first one. It was from Petunia Pretty Paws.

"G, Good luck organizing the grand opening. See you there!" it read.

I had no idea what Petunia was talking about, but just thinking about her made me smile. She is such a special mouse. She's smart and kind and funny and **pretty** and . . .

Without even realizing it, I started to doodle her name over and over on a piece of paper.

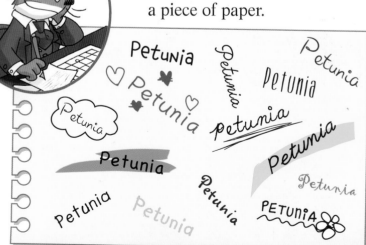

I'll Do It!

Suddenly, Trap burst into my office.

"Hey, Cuz! I'm heading off for a little R and R on RAT ISLAND this week, so I need that suit for the grand opening **pronto**," he squeaked.

That did it! I had to find out what was going on!

"What **grand opening**? What are you talking about?" I shrieked.

Trap looked surprised. For some strange reason he wouldn't look me in the **EYE**. "Uh, you mean you don't know about the grand opening?" he muttered. Then he turned **WHITE**, then **RED**, then **PURPLE**.

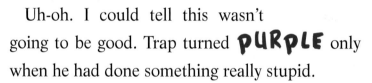

Uh-oh. I could tell this wasn't going to be good. Trap turned **PURPLE** only when he had done something really stupid.

Two minutes later I found out what it was. It was worse than I'd thought!

It seemed a month earlier, while I was away on vacation, Trap had thrown a **wild** party at my house. In the middle of the party my friend Dr. Karina von Fossisnout, the **DIRECTOR** of the Mouseum of Natural History, had called my home and spoken with Trap. She had broken her leg on an expedition and wanted to know if I could step in and organize the grand opening of the **DRAGON EXHIBIT** at the mouseum.

"Of course I told her **no problem-o!** I knew you'd want to help, right, Germeister?" Trap explained.

I was ready to **EXPLODE.** First, why was Trap throwing **parties** at my house while I was away? And second, though I wanted to help Karina, I didn't know the first thing about **DRAGONS!**

"So when is this grand opening taking place?" I asked worriedly.

Trap clapped me on the back so hard I heard my teeth **rattle**.

"Don't worry, Gerbaby, you've got a whole week to pull this thing together!" he announced.

A WEEK?!!

I felt faint. A grand opening at the New Mouse City **MOUSEUM OF NATURAL HISTORY** is usually a huge affair!

I'd need to **print** flyers, write the program, **ORGANIZE** the dedication ceremony, arrange the buffet tables, *order* floral decorations and . . .

Cheese niblets! I felt sick. There was no way I could manage it all.

Just then I noticed the paper I had been doodling on. **Petunia!** I couldn't disappoint her!

So I stood on my chair, held my ruler in the air, and squeaked:

"I'LL DO IT!"

What else could I say?

SOB! SOB! SOB!

Once I decided to take on the dragon project, there was no time to waste. I had so much to do. First I made a list.

Rancid rat hairs! It was a mile long!

My head felt like it was about to explode. There was no way I could get all the things on the list done in a week's time. I began to sob uncontrollably. Sob! Sob! Sob!

My secretary, Mousella, stuck her head in the door. "Anything wrong, boss?" she asked.

How embarrassing!

After Mousella left, I gave myself a pep talk. *Don't be a wimp! You can do it!* I told myself. I looked at my list. **#1: Write program.** Piece of cake! I loved writing. Too bad I was writing about **DRAGONS**. I didn't know the first thing about them.

I **RAN** to the library to do research — lots of research. I was there until closing.

What an exhausting night!

On **Saturday** I did more **research** on the Internet.

FRIDAY

On **Sunday** I put together my notes for the dedication ceremony.

On **Monday** I booked the caterers.

On **Tuesday** I ordered the flowers.

SATURDAY

On **Wednesday** I consulted the mouseum director.

On **Thursday** I hired the musicians.

On **Friday** I delivered the finished program and flyers to the printer.

SUNDAY

MONDAY

TUESDAY

Finally, one night before the big opening, everything was **finished**!

Cheesecake! I was so tired my whole body ached . . . even my **fur**! I thanked everyone in the office who had helped me. Then I **dragged** myself home.

But when I **CLIMBED** into my bed, I couldn't fall asleep. I kept thinking about the dragon exhibit. Would the flyers look nice? What about the *flowers*? Would there be enough food at the reception? I just couldn't stop worrying.

At last I drifted off. But then I dreamed I was being chased by dragons! **HELP!**

When my alarm clock **rang** the next morning, I had barely slept a wink!

WEDNESDAY

THURSDAY

FRIDAY

Oh, if only I could sleep the whole day **long**! But I had to get to the mouseum.

With a groan, I **dragged** myself into the bathroom. **Putrid cheese puffs!** I hardly recognized my reflection in the mirror. I looked like I'd just seen *Return of the Killer Cats*, the most **HORRIFYING** movie of all time! My fur was **sticking** up all over the place. And there were **DARK** circles around my eyes.

Still, somehow I managed to SHOWER, eat, and get dressed in record time.

WHO KNEW WHY?

When I arrived at the mouseum, **Frederick Fuzzypaws**, the mayor of New Mouse City, was waiting for me. We shook paws. We talked about the weather, my books, and other things. I must admit, I was so tired from lack of sleep, my brain felt like mashed potatoes!

I did notice, though, that as we were speaking, several mice were staring at me strangely.

Who knew why?

I tried to pretend not to notice. But I was starting to feel terribly self-conscious. Everywhere I looked, beady little eyes stared back at me.

It was driving me crazy!

Just when I thought things couldn't get any worse . . .

(1) I TRIPPED on the carpet and, while

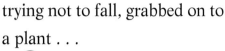

trying not to fall, grabbed on to a plant . . .

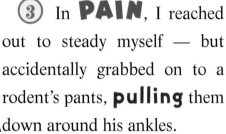

② which was actually a cactus with RAZOR-SHARP needles!

③ In **PAIN**, I reached out to steady myself — but accidentally grabbed on to a rodent's pants, **pulling** them down around his ankles.

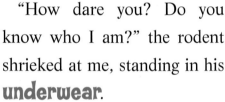

"How dare you? Do you know who I am?" the rodent shrieked at me, standing in his **underwear**.

I stared down at my paws, embarrassed, and that was when I noticed something even more **humiliating**. I was still wearing my **SLIPPERS**, and instead of a shirt, I had on my

pajama top! So that was why everyone was **STARING** at me!

Right then it was time for my speech, so I stuck my slippers into my pocket and SCAMPERED to the podium. To be honest, I don't remember much about the rest of the night. I was so tired! I do remember that **Karina von Fossisnout** thanked me (what a good friend!), **Sally Ratmousen** complimented me on my shirt (my pajama top!), and I ate too much at the buffet (**BURP!**).

Very bizarre...

Nice shirt!

Thanks!

Well done, Grandson!

OH, WHEN WOULD I LEARN?

That evening I **dragged** myself home. I was so exhausted that as soon as my head hit the pillow, I was out like a **light**. But in the middle of the night, I woke up tossing and turning. I had a terrible **stomachache**.

Oh, when would I learn not to stuff myself like **Uncle Cheesebelly** at the Stilton Family Cheddarfest!

I **STUMBLED** out of bed and flung open the window. Maybe a little fresh air would do me some good.

Oh, how it burns!

Then I made myself a cup of chamomile tea but **spilled** some on my paw by accident. "**YOUCH!**" I squeaked. I had forgotten all about my sore paw. Those cactus needles had really done a number on it. Now it was **THROBBING** even more!

Let's try this. . . .

I tried **BLOWING** on it, running it under some cold water, and even packing it in **ice**. Nothing worked. Oh, why couldn't I have touched a nice **soft** fern instead of a cactus with a bazillion **SHARP** needles?!!!

Ouch, it hurts so much!

At dawn, I fell asleep. I dreamed I was swimming in the ocean. The sun was WARM. Gentle waves soothed my paw.

The smell of roses filled the air. Roses? At the beach?

I opened my eyes. I saw a long pink tongue licking my paw, and two enormouse amber-colored eyes.

It was the Dragon of the Rainbow and my froggy friend Scribblehopper!

They are from the Kingdom of Fantasy.

"Why are you here?" I asked.

The Dragon of the Rainbow, who has a habit of **singing** when he speaks, sang out:

"We have come at Sterling's request —
oh, brave knight, you are the best!
You are honest, true, and kind
and possess a brilliant mind.
Plus you hold the Fire Brand,
which will help you in our land.
Only you can stop the fight
and make the Land of Dragons right!"

I must admit I liked the bit about my brilliant mind. But the Kingdom of Fantasy folk always insisted on calling me a KNIGHT, against my protests. And the rest of the song made no sense to me!

TO THE RAINBOW!

"What FIRE BRAND?" I mumbled.

Scribblehopper giggled. "Oh, Sir Knight, don't be so modest! The mark King Firebreath III put on your paw on your first trip to the Kingdom of Fantasy. Remember?"

I looked at my paw and saw that my webbed friend was right. I had the Fire Brand STAMPED on it. No wonder it BURNED so much!

Suddenly, everything that had happened on my very first adventure to THE KINGDOM OF FANTASY came rushing back to me. Meeting Cackle, the TERRIFYING Queen of the Witches, and Blossom, the kindhearted Queen of the Fairies. I stared into space, remembering.

Scribblehopper cleared his throat loudly. "Uh, I hate to cut into your daydream, Your **Knightliness**, but we'd better get hopping. Sterling, the Princess of the Silver Dragons, has

---

FIRE BRAND

Firebreath III, the King of the Dragons of Fire, set this mark on Geronimo's paw during his first voyage to the Kingdom of Fantasy. It showed that Geronimo was traveling through the kingdom with the permission of King Firebreath. An ancient prophecy says that one day a knight will save all the dragons, and his palm will bear a mark similar to this one, but made of **blue light**.

requested your presence at the **GREAT COUNCIL OF THE TWELVE DRAGONS**. So lose the pj's and let's hit it!"

On my last voyage to the Kingdom of Fantasy, Sterling had helped me save **Blossom**. Now she needed my help.

I was dying to catch a few **Z's**. But what could I do? I had to go.

So I put on my armor, mounted the dragon, and squeaked: "To the rainbow!"

IN THE KINGDOM
OF THE SILVER
DRAGONS

Me? A Hero?

We flew through the sky, made **golden** by the dawn. I have to say, it really is an amazing sight — even for a scaredy-mouse like me. (Did I mention I'm afraid of heights?) If I unclasped my paw from the dragon's back, it felt as if I could touch the stars! Of course, I would never do anything **CRAZY** like that.

I thought about Sterling. "Are you sure she wants *my* help?" I asked Scribblehopper.

The frog **croaked**, "Of course! You've got the Fire Brand. You're the **HERO** of the story!"

My whiskers trembled. Me? A hero? I started thinking about the scary creatures I might encounter: MONSTERS, WITCHES, OGRES . . .

By the time we entered the Kingdom of Fantasy, I was a wreck! Then things got worse. Down below, it was autumn—but in the Kingdom of Fantasy, it's supposed to be eternally spring!

Later I spotted an even more TERRIFYING sight.

A huge fire was about to burn up the TALKING FOREST!

As the Dragon of the Rainbow swooped down

lower, I spotted the **DARK SHADOWS** of three dragons fleeing the area.

Could they have started the **FIRE**? Had it been an accident?

Maybe they had just been **roasting** marshmallows and their campfire had gotten out of control. That got me thinking about toasted **marshmallows**. *Mmmm, delicious*, I thought.

Just then I heard a desperate cry.

"HELP! FIRE! SAVE US!!!"

We landed just outside the circle of fire. The **heat** and the **smoke** were unbearable! We

began to *choke* and cough.

I racked my brain, trying to think of a way to put out the fire, Oh, where was a good **fire extinguisher** when you needed one?

Right then I heard a voice. "Hurry, Knight! We're the first row of trees. If you **KNOCK** us down, the flames won't spread any farther!"

I looked around. A giant **blue** tree waved a branch at me. "Over here!" he shouted.

I felt terrible. How could I destroy a BEAUTIFUL living tree?!

The tree noticed my hesitation, and said, "Don't worry. We've been around for hundreds of years and we've dropped tons of SEEDS. There'll be new SEEDLINGS sprouting UP in no time!"

I felt awful about

knocking down the trees, but what could I do? The flames were **spreading** faster than a pack of rats at a free cheddar tasting.

"Okay," I said. Then I gave the command and the Dragon of the Rainbow knocked DOWN the trees with his mighty tail.

WHOMP!

Meanwhile, Scribblehopper and I tried our best to put out the rest of the burning FLAMES.

It wasn't easy. Scribblehopper tried snuffing out the flames with his jacket. I, on the other paw, picked up a bunch of green leafy tree branches.

Singed . . .

Roasted . . .

Cooked to perfection!

SMACK! SMACK! SMACK!

I pounded the branches on the fire with all my might, which unfortunately wasn't much. Did I happen to mention I'm not the most **ATHLETIC** mouse on the block? Finally, after what felt like a **million years**, we put the very last ember out.

When we finished, my whiskers were SINGED, my fur was roasted, and my paws were like two lumps of grilled cheese cooked to perfection!

Scribblehopper took one look at me and burst out laughing.

"Sorry, Sir Knight. You're looking a little fried," he confessed.

I was about to tell my froggy friend that he didn't

look so great himself, when a voice interrupted my thoughts.

"Thanks for saving us!"

I waved good-bye to the **talking** trees as we took off for the

Kingdom of the Silver Dragons.

Twenty minutes later, the dragon shouted, **"Brace yoursssselvessssss!!!"**

We landed in front of a tree with **silvery** leaves. It was Sterling's palace.

1. CRYSTAL CAVES
2. STERLING'S PALACE
3. SECRET PASSAGE
4. DIVING BOARD
5. DRAGON LAKE
6. SILVER RIVER
7. NURSERY
8. ROCK BRIDGE
9. HOSPITAL
10. OUTDOOR THEATER
11. GYM
12. CONTROL TOWER
13. ARENA FOR COMPETITIONS
14. LANDING AREA
15. LIBRARY

In the Kingdom of the Silver Dragons

Just then we heard the sound of beating wings. Sparkle, Sterling's dragon, swooped down and landed in front of us, calling,

"Welcome to the Kingdom of the Silver Dragons!"

Sparkle,
Sterling's dragon

Sterling

THE PRINCESS OF THE SILVER DRAGONS

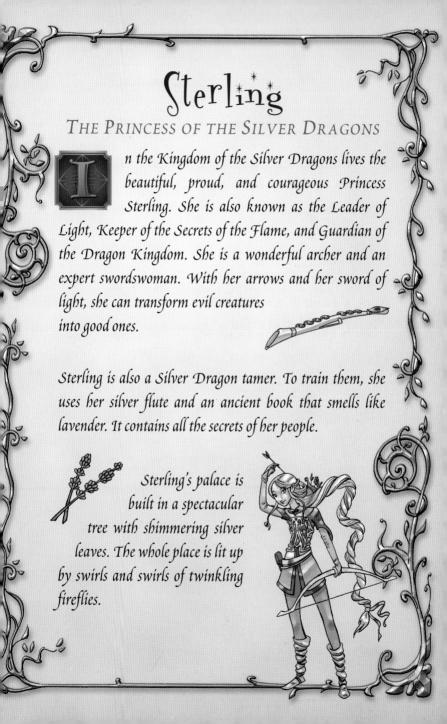

I n the Kingdom of the Silver Dragons lives the beautiful, proud, and courageous Princess Sterling. She is also known as the Leader of Light, Keeper of the Secrets of the Flame, and Guardian of the Dragon Kingdom. She is a wonderful archer and an expert swordswoman. With her arrows and her sword of light, she can transform evil creatures into good ones.

Sterling is also a Silver Dragon tamer. To train them, she uses her silver flute and an ancient book that smells like lavender. It contains all the secrets of her people.

Sterling's palace is built in a spectacular tree with shimmering silver leaves. The whole place is lit up by swirls and swirls of twinkling fireflies.

"Let's let the *Dragon of the Rainbow* rest while I take you to see Sterling," she suggested.

Beside me, Scribblehopper began hopping **UP** and **down** like a crazed fan at a **Twisted Tails** concert.

"Can you believe it, Sir Knight?" he squeaked. "She's taking us **inside** the palace! We're the first **OUTSIDERS** allowed in! I think I will compose a poem to **celebrate** the occasion!"

I **GULPED**. Have you ever read one of Scribblehopper's poems? If you have, you might not remember it. That's because there's a good chance that you fell **ASLEEP** before you made

it through the whole thing!

Yep, that frog is one **wordy** amphibian!

Luckily, I convinced him to put his pen down. "We shouldn't keep the princess waiting," I insisted.

"You're right, *Sir Geronimo of Stilton*," Scribblehopper agreed. "I will compose my literary **MASTERPIECE** later, when I have more time. Then I can make it extra, extra, extra **long**!"

I stifled a **groan**.

Soon we were perched on Sparkle's back, headed toward Sterling. Below, I heard Sterling's flute playing a **sad** tune.

How strange. It was not like her to get discouraged easily. A **bad** feeling came over me.

Oh, how I wished I were only *dreaming*!

I Hate to
Tell You . . .

Sparkle set us down under a tangle of silver trees. What a sight! The whole place was lit up by **blinking** fireflies swirling around in tiny **circles** of twinkling lights.

Sterling sat in an enormouse SILVER throne. Her blonde hair seemed to *glow* along with the fireflies overhead.

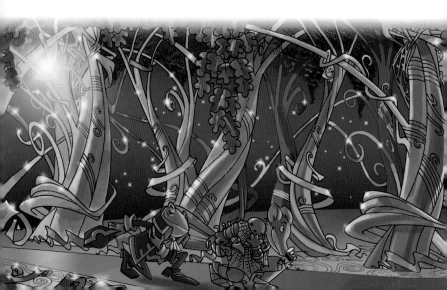

Slowly, we approached the throne and **BOWED** before the princess.

"Oh, Princess," I squeaked. "I hate to tell you this, but someone tried to burn down the TALKING FOREST. And autumn is here — the leaves are **dried** out. Something terrible is going on!"

The princess nodded sadly. "I was afraid this might happen. I called you because Blossom entrusted me with the last existing **dragon egg**, and it's been stolen! But now I see that the situation is even **worse** than I thought."

PING

PONG

She sighed, then said, "But that's enough talking for now, Knight. I am sure you are tired from your long journey. My faithful aides, **PING** and **PONG**, will take good care of you."

Sterling was right. I was tired. But I was dying to hear more about the *missing* dragon egg! Still, I didn't want to upset her, so I stayed **QUIET**.

Suddenly, Sterling clapped her hands and we heard **LOUD** footsteps. . . .

Badaboom! *Badaboom!* *Badaboom!*
Badaboom! *Badaboom!* *Badaboom!*
Badaboom! *Badaboom!* *Badaboom!*

Two dragons entered the room. One was very THIN, with a neck like a giraffe and a sweet light voice. The other was very FAT, with a belly like a hot-air balloon and a voice so DEEP it seemed to come from inside a cave. They rubbed their paws together and said, "Get ready for the one . . . the only . . . the famous . . . DRAGONS' WELCOME!"

PING let Scribblehopper climb onto his back. PONG, on the other hand, grabbed me by the tail. I squeaked in terror, but for some reason, he pretended not to notice.

Put me down!

NIGHTY NIGHT, KNIGHT!

With a mighty flap of his wings, Pong took off. I **dangled** from his claws and tried not to **lose** my lunch. Stinky cheese sticks! We were high up. Did I mention I'm afraid of heights, **sharp** claws, and the sound a garbage truck makes when it backs up? But that's another story. . . .

Anyway, where was I? Oh, yes, to keep myself calm, I imagined the welcome the dragons had planned. Of course there would be **TONS** of food, a *warm* comfortable bed, and maybe even a hot **steamy** bubble bath . . . my favorite!

Too bad that was all only in my imagination.

A short while later, Pong set me down. Then he flung open a **gray** door and exclaimed, "Here's your room! Nighty night, Knight!"

The room was **cold** and dark and reminded me of a PRISON CELL. Where was the comfy bed? Where was the welcoming **cheese platter**?

Pong handed me an alarm clock shaped like a dragon. "Tomorrow, wake up at 5:00 A.M. sharp! The **Dragons' Welcome Program** begins at 5:01!" he roared.

I tried not to cry. I didn't want to offend the dragon, but I am so not a **morning mouse**!

Plus, I was completely exhausted!

With a TINY wave to Pong, I closed the door behind me. Oh, well. At least I wouldn't have any problems falling asleep. Once my head hit the pillow, I'd be out.

I SLUMPED over to the bed and sat down. And that was when I made a terrible discovery:

The bed was made of **STONE**!
I patted the pillow. **Youch!**
The pillow was made of
STONE!

The sheets were made of **STONE**!
The nightstand was made of
STONE!

Even the flowers were made of
STONE!

Still, what could I do? I was so, so tired. I curled up into a ball and cried myself to sleep. Soon I was **snoring** away.

But just as I was starting to have a wonderful dream involving yours truly and a deliciously cheesy pizza pie, a voice screeched,

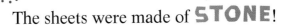

"WAKE UUUUUUUP!"

An instant later a powerful FLAME almost burned my tail to a crisp!

It was the dragon alarm. Time to get up. As I headed for the door, I noticed a basket of fruit. I would have loved an **omelet**, but I was starving. I grabbed an **APPLE** and took a bite.

Crack!

Rats!

I should have known. The apple was made of **STONE**!

CRACK!

I thought about calling a dentist. Had I **chipped** my tooth? But just then Pong arrived at my room.

"**You're late!**" he shrieked, grabbing me by the ear. A moment later we were flying above an enormouse stone basin that had clouds of steam coming out of it.

"Here we are, Knight. Our first stop in the

Helllllllp!

DRAGONS' Welcome Program: the **thermal** bath!" he declared.

"**NOOOO!**" I cried as he dropped me snoutfirst into the STEAMING water below.

I mean, don't get me wrong. I love a nice hot bubble bath. But this one was so hot it was **boiling**!

Unfortunately, Pong just ignored my cries for help. Instead, he left me there in the SCALDING hot water for half an hour. By the time he came back to get me, my fur was as

red as a fully cooked lobster!

Then, without giving me time to protest, he threw me into a tub of **freezing** cold water. There were even blocks of ice floating around.

"**T-t-ooo c-c-c-c-old!**" I chattered.

But once again Pong ignored me.

Oh, what a nightmare!

Eventually, after what seemed like ten million **years**, Pong returned. When he took me out, my fur was **frozen solid**. I felt just like a giant

Frozen Flounder!

Just when I thought it couldn't get any worse, Pong picked me up and dumped me into a stone tub filled with **stinky** mud. I was covered from head to paw!

Yuck!

Then he threw me under a **roaring** waterfall.

Yikes, that hurt!

Owwww!!!!

Next he locked me in a dark cave filled with **steam**.

And finally, he insisted on giving me a back **RUB**. Aaayiii! It felt more like a back **SLAM**!

Oh, how much longer was this Dragons' Welcome Program going to be?

I wasn't sure I would last one more second!

BAD MOVE!

With a **groan**, I sat down on the stone steps. My head was **pounding**, and I **ached** from head to paw. Oh, how I wished I were home in my cozy mouse hole!

The weirdest thing was that I couldn't figure out why the dragons were treating me so badly. I had traveled all the way to the **KINGDOM OF**

Sigh. I want to go home!

FANTASY just to help them. And now instead of welcoming me, it was as if they were trying to TORTURE me. I was feeling so BLUE I almost started bawling.

At that exact moment, I felt someone **tapping** me on the shoulder. It was Ping and Pong. They had huge smiles on their faces. Suddenly, they burst out laughing.

*6 HA HA HA! HO HO HO!
HEE HEE HEE!
HA HA HA! HO HO HO!9*

Have you ever heard a dragon **LAUGH**? Let me tell you, it is extremely contagious. Before I knew it, I began laughing my **fur** off and I had no idea why!

When I finally caught my BREATH, I turned to Pong. "I hope you don't think I'm **Dense**,"

I began. "But why are you laughing so hard?"

Pong grinned. "We are just happy for you, Knight. You passed the **test**!" he declared.

Then Ping explained that they had come up with the **DRAGONS' WELCOME PROGRAM** to see if I was **worthy**.

"Since the **dragon egg** was stolen, we don't trust anyone," Pong added.

"We needed to know you'd respect us and our customs even if they were a little . . . harsh."

A little harsh? I thought. Didn't he mean **TORTUROUS**?!

As he was talking, I noticed Pong was looking at me with a **STRANGE** expression. Just then, he began to whisper **excitedly** in Ping's ear.

"Psst . . . psst . . . psst . . . **PROPHECY** . . . psst . . . psst . . . psst . . . **TWELFTH KNIGHT**."

Then they turned to me and **chanted**:

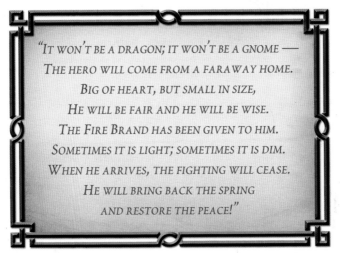

"IT WON'T BE A DRAGON; IT WON'T BE A GNOME —
THE HERO WILL COME FROM A FARAWAY HOME.
BIG OF HEART, BUT SMALL IN SIZE,
HE WILL BE FAIR AND HE WILL BE WISE.
THE FIRE BRAND HAS BEEN GIVEN TO HIM.
SOMETIMES IT IS LIGHT; SOMETIMES IT IS DIM.
WHEN HE ARRIVES, THE FIGHTING WILL CEASE.
HE WILL BRING BACK THE SPRING
AND RESTORE THE PEACE!"

When they were done, they continued staring at me **INTENSELY**. *Okay, this is weird, I* thought. To be honest, the chanting they'd done had sort of CREEPED ME OUT. What did it mean?

When I asked, Pong brushed me off.

"Talk to Sterling," he said. "She's waiting for you at the banquet hall." Then he placed me onto his back and we took off into the sky. It was so cloudy I could barely see my own whiskers! Immediately, I began to panic. What if we crashed into something?!

Luckily, we reached the banquet hall in one piece. It was located at the top of the tree that held Sterling's palace. Yikes! I was going to have to eat so high up in a tree?!

Still, what could I do? I couldn't leave now. I was STARVING!

I looked around. The room was incredible. The whole place sparkled. It was packed with dragons of every age and of every color. They were all chattering away until they spotted me.

Then they began WHiSPERiNg.

Normally, I would be **emBaRRaSSeD**, but I was too hungry to care.

At the appetizer table I grabbed a glass filled with a strange **red** liquid. I drank it down in one gulp. **Bad move!** It was tomato juice seasoned with SPICY peppers!

To calm the burning, I stuffed a pawful of appetizers into my mouth. **Worse move!** They were filled with RED-HOT pepper flakes!

Desperate, I spotted a pitcher of something. It wasn't red, so I knew it wasn't tomato juice. I chugged down the entire contents. **The worst move ever!** It was pure HOT-pepper oil!

HOLEY CHEESE, WAS THAT PEPPER SPICY!

Tears ran down my fur and **FIRE** shot out of my mouth.

Right at that moment, a dragon dressed like a butler **rang** a small bell. "**Lunch is served!**" he announced. Then he proudly read the menu aloud.

APPETIZER
TOMATO SOUP WITH
SPICY PEPPERS
~
SALAD
FRESH SPINACH WITH
SPICY PEPPERS
~
ENTRÉES
PASTA WITH SPICY PEPPERS

CHICKEN CUTLETS WITH
SPICY PEPPERS

SIRLOIN STEAK WITH
SPICY PEPPERS
~
SIDE
GRILLED SPICY PEPPERS
~
DESSERT
SPICE CAKE WITH SPICY PEPPERS

My eyes felt like they were about to pop out of my **fur**! If I ate one more spicy pepper, I would **EXPLODE**!

"Um, sorry to bother you," I said to the butler. "But do you happen to have a glass of **cold** water?"

He shot me a look. "WATER?!!" he roared. **"WHAT'S WRONG WITH MY MENU?"**

I didn't think it would be a good idea to tell a dragon that I didn't like **spicy red peppers**. What if he breathed fire on me? So I stayed silent.

Luckily, Sterling arrived just then and ordered me a bunch of delicious food fit for a mouse.

OH, HOW I LOVE MY CHEESE!

THE TWELFTH KNIGHT

After I was done **stuffing** my face, Sterling took me aside. She touched the Fire Brand on my paw. It lit up with a **blue light**.

"I knew it!" she exclaimed. "The Fire Brand has become the **Brand of Light**! You are the Twelfth Knight. You will find the lost **egg** and restore **peace** to our land!"

Restore **peace**? I couldn't even get my cousin Trap and my sister, Thea, to get along!

But now Sterling had her own story to tell. It was **THE PROPHECY OF THE TWELFTH KNIGHT**.

After she was done telling her story, Sterling

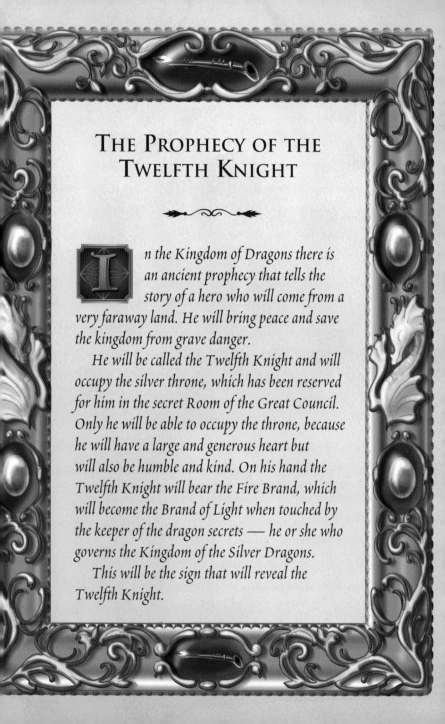

THE PROPHECY OF THE TWELFTH KNIGHT

I n the Kingdom of Dragons there is an ancient prophecy that tells the story of a hero who will come from a very faraway land. He will bring peace and save the kingdom from grave danger.

He will be called the Twelfth Knight and will occupy the silver throne, which has been reserved for him in the secret Room of the Great Council. Only he will be able to occupy the throne, because he will have a large and generous heart but will also be humble and kind. On his hand the Twelfth Knight will bear the Fire Brand, which will become the Brand of Light when touched by the keeper of the dragon secrets — he or she who governs the Kingdom of the Silver Dragons.

This will be the sign that will reveal the Twelfth Knight.

stood up and said, "Let the Great Dragon Council begin!"

TOOT TURU TOOO!
TOOT TURU TOO!
TOOT TURU TOOO!

Immediately, a thousand **silver** trumpets sounded. Sterling motioned for me to follow her.

"You must also participate in the **Great Dragon Council**. It is our custom to call it to order every time there are **serious** problems in the two dragon kingdoms or if someone has violated one of the laws in the ancient Dragons' Code," she explained.

THE TWO DRAGON KINGDOMS

In the Kingdom of Fantasy there are two dragon kingdoms. One is the Kingdom of the Silver Dragons, which is governed by Sterling. The other is the Kingdom of the Fire Dragons, which is governed by King Firebreath III.

I hated to leave the banquet room. There were still plates piled **high** with cheddar slices I hadn't eaten! **RATS!**

The dragons rushed along a **long**, **dark** corridor. Sterling turned to me and whispered, "We have to go through a secret passageway to get to the SECReT meeting room. The members of the Great Council are the only ones who know about it."

By now, my heart was pounding. Everything was so **MYSTERIOUS**. We entered the throne room and stood before the third column. Then Sterling pulled a HiDDeN handle on the column. The floor opened up to reveal a long spiral staircase that went down . . . **DOWN** . . . **DOWN** . . . **DOWN** . . . **DOWN** . . . **DOWN** . . .

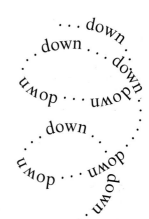

. . . down
down . . . down
. . down . . . down
down . . . down
. . down
down
. down . . down
down
. . .

THE GREAT COUNCIL
OF TWELVE DRAGONS

When at last I reached the secret room, I looked around for a place to sit. I noticed that the seat opposite Sterling was empty. On the backrest of the chair was an engraving written in the FANTASIAN ALPHABET.* Here it is! Can you translate it?

I was about to sit down when a dragon **grabbed** me roughly by the tail.

76

* You can find the Fantasian Alphabet on page 311.

"Can't you read, Knight?" a cold voice **SNARLED**.

I turned and saw it was King Firebreath III. He was so annoyed he **SCRATCHED** the table and broke a nail.

"Now look what you made me do!" he **ROARED**. It was then that I noticed that his wrist was in a bandage and he sounded a little stuffed up, like he had a cold.

FIREBREATH III

Firebreath III, the King of the Dragons of Fire, is famous for having a quick temper.

Geronimo met him on his very first trip to the Kingdom of Fantasy. It was Firebreath who gave Geronimo the Fire Brand.

Was that why he was so *CRANKY*?

At that moment I realized what the Fantasian sentence on the chair said: Here sits the Twelfth Knight.

OOPS! I hadn't realized it was a reserved seat. But when I looked around to find another spot, I discovered every chair was taken.

Right then Sterling stood up and **glared** at Firebreath. "How dare you speak to the knight in this way!" she scolded. "He is the **Twelfth**! Can't you tell?"

Then I remembered the story Sterling had told me earlier. She said *I* was the TWELFTH KNIGHT!

Firebreath stepped aside.

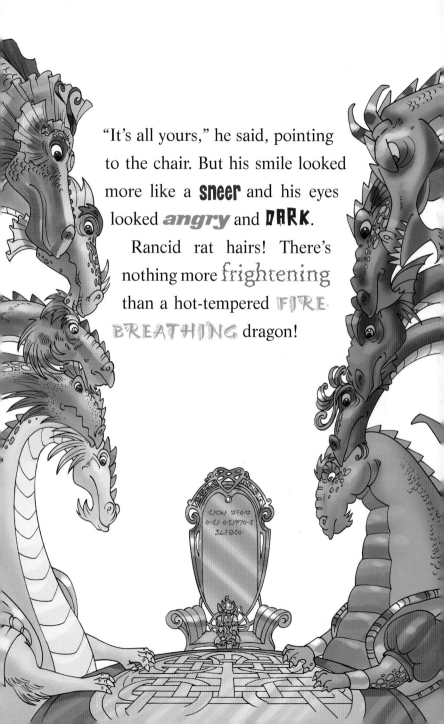

"It's all yours," he said, pointing to the chair. But his smile looked more like a **sneer** and his eyes looked *angry* and **DARK**.

Rancid rat hairs! There's nothing more frightening than a hot-tempered FIRE-BREATHING dragon!

WHO? WHO? WHO?

I was trying not to think about Firebreath when Sterling **clapped** her hands to get everyone's attention. "Friends, I would like to introduce you to our long-awaited, brave, and kind **Twelfth Knight**!" she said.

Feeling shy, I waved my paw at everyone.

The dragons **roared** their welcome (all of them except Firebreath).

ROARRRR!

Then they *braided* their tails together (all of them except Firebreath).

Finally, they put their **paws** together (all of them except Firebreath).

Sterling continued talking

in a serious voice. "Dear COURAGEOUS knight and trusted **silver** and FIRE dragons, I'm afraid I must tell you some terrible news. The last **dragon egg** has been stolen!" she announced.

The room erupted in loud gasps. The dragons were in **shock**.

"The **egg**? The very last one?" said one dragon.

"But **who** could have stolen it?" said another.

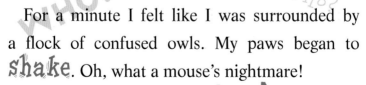

Who? Who? Who?
Who? Who? Who?
Who? Who? Who?
Who? Who? Who?

For a minute I felt like I was surrounded by a flock of confused owls. My paws began to shake. Oh, what a mouse's nightmare!

Luckily, Sterling's voice broke into my thoughts. "The dragon egg was given to me by

Blossom, the **Queen of the Fairies**," she explained. "I was to watch over it until it hatched. As you know, it is our most precious **treasure**, since only one dragon is born every **thousand** years. If it were to be destroyed, dragons could become extinct and the balance of the Kingdom of Fantasy would be **broken**."

She shook her head sadly. "The thing that hurts me the most is that only you, members of the Great Council, know about the ꙅecꝛet passage to reach the cave where the egg was hidden," she murmured.

Slowly Sterling stared with **penetrating** eyes at each dragon seated around the table. "There is a **traitor** among us!" she proclaimed.

At this all the dragons gasped again — everyone except Firebreath. He just stared back at Sterling with a **strange** expression on his face. Then he said in a slimy voice, "Be that as it may, Sterling, **YOU** still must now obey **THE DRAGON LAWS**. **YOU** have failed Blossom. **YOU** have lost the egg. Now **YOU** must leave the kingdom."

> ### TRAITOR
> A traitor is someone who betrays someone else's trust. For example, if you promised a friend you would help her study for a spelling contest, but instead you helped her smartest competitor study for the contest, she would view you as a traitor.

Then he began to read aloud from a very old book.

"The Dragon Laws state: *He or she who is not worthy of keeping command must leave the kingdom within seven days and never return again!*"

I couldn't believe Firebreath wanted Sterling **gone**!

"I'll help you find the egg, Princess," I told her.

THE DRAGON LAWS

1. EVERY DRAGON MUST RECOGNIZE BLOSSOM, THE QUEEN OF THE FAIRIES, AS THE SUPREME QUEEN OF THE KINGDOM OF FANTASY.

2. EVERY DRAGON PROMISES TO FIGHT CACKLE, THE QUEEN OF THE WITCHES.

3. EVERY DRAGON MUST SWEAR LOYALTY TO THE RULER OF THE KINGDOM IN WHICH HE OR SHE LIVES AND MUST OBEY THE SUPREME AUTHORITY OF THE GREAT COUNCIL.

4. THE GREAT COUNCIL UNITES THE RULERS OF THE KINGDOM OF THE SILVER DRAGONS AND THE KINGDOM OF THE FIRE DRAGONS WITH NINE OTHER WISE AND NOBLE DRAGONS . . . AND WITH THE TWELFTH KNIGHT, WHEN AND IF HE ARRIVES.

5. THE GREAT COUNCIL MEETS WHEN THERE IS THREAT OF DANGER IN EITHER OF THE DRAGON KINGDOMS.

6. THE OBLIGATION OF EVERY DRAGON IS TO DEFEND THE EGG: THE FUTURE OF THE DRAGONS DEPENDS ON IT!

7. HE OR SHE WHO IS NOT WORTHY OF KEEPING COMMAND MUST LEAVE THE KINGDOM WITHIN SEVEN DAYS AND NEVER RETURN AGAIN!

Sterling smiled gratefully. "Such a brave knight!" she said.

I gulped. Actually, I wasn't brave. I was a scaredy-mouse! But I had to do what was right.

I'll help you!

A SECRET
PASSAGEWAY

Sterling stood **up** and addressed the table. "I will respect the Dragon Laws. If within **one week** I cannot find the lost egg and prove I am a **worthy** leader, I will leave the kingdom forever. That is all. The Great Council is adjourned!"

I was about to leave when Sterling whispered for me to follow her.

She led me to her private living room, which had a table full of food: whisker-licking-good cheesecake, **cheddar Danish**, and hunks of fresh Swiss. I tried not to stuff my snout, but everything was so **DELICIOUS** I couldn't stop myself! I ate and ate and ate.

When I finally looked up from my plate, I saw Sterling staring at me. I tried to thank her for the

food, but I accidentally let out a **burp** instead. Oh, how *embarrassing*!

After I excused myself, Sterling said, "Knight, you are a **true friend**. I just know you will be able to find the lost **egg**. But first I must tell you where it was before it was stolen. There is a SeCReT passageway leading to a SeCReT underground room. Through the SeCReT underground room is the SeCReT cave where the dragon egg was hidden."

I shivered. I didn't know if I could handle all these SeCReTS. But I didn't want to tell Sterling . . . so I kept it a SeCReT.

YEP, ANOTHER SECRET!

Sterling led me back to the Great Council room. She pressed a secret **BUTTON** (yep, another SeCReT!) on the arm of her chair, and immediately, the table in the middle of the room began to sink. We quickly jumped on top of it, and before you could say "squeak," we arrived in a mysterious underground room.

Pong was waiting for us.

"Pong will lead you to the secret cave. Good luck!" Sterling said before she left. It was so DARK. I was scared out of my fur. But then things got even SCARIER! To keep the cave's location a secret, ① first Pong blindfolded me. ② Then he SPUN me around a thousand times. ③ Finally, he made me cover my ears.

He blindfolded me . . .

. . . he spun me around . . .

. . . and he made me cover my ears!

By now I was so *dizzy* I felt like I had spent the day *tumbling* around in a giant clothes dryer! All I could figure out was that we were moving farther underground and that it was getting **colder**.

Eventually we stopped. I felt some kind of a rock wall in front of me. It was SMOOTH and as **cold** as **ice**.

"How do we get past this wall?" I asked Pong.

Of course, I couldn't exactly hear his answer, since my paws were covering my ears. But I thought I heard him say something about a SECRET PASSWORD.

A minute later Pong took the blindfold off my eyes (and I took my paws off my ears) and I saw there was now an opening in the wall.

"This is it. The entrance to the cave of the **dragon's egg**," he explained. "You go ahead and investigate and I will meet you at the exit on the other side. Don't forget to put the blindfold back on when you come out. The cave exit is an ancient dragon SECRET."

As I headed into the **MYSTERIOUS** opening in the wall, I wondered if my brain would be able to keep track of all these ancient dragon SECRETS! Holey cheese, there were a ton of them!

Still, there was no time to worry about it. Soon I reached an enormouse **CAVE** with glowing green walls.

The cave was carved in **dragolite**, the mysterious **DRAGON** stone. . . .

What a sight!

Dragolite

Dragolite is an extremely rare stone with incredible properties. It can be found only in the dragon kingdoms. It keeps the temperature consistent, which is why caves of dragolite are the most suited for holding dragon eggs. Dragon doctors also use it to cure a hoarse throat, treat a cold or cough, and calm a nervous dragon.

STERLING'S PALACE IN THE
KINGDOM OF THE SILVER DRAGONS:
A MYSTERIOUS BUILDING

THE THREE ANCIENT DRAGON SECRETS:

First Dragon Secret: In Sterling's throne room there is a secret passageway to the Great Council Room. Just pull the curly silver handle at the bottom of the third column.

Second Dragon Secret: In the Great Council Room there is a secret passageway to a mysterious underground room. Just push the button on the right armrest of Sterling's chair, and the table sinks down to it.

Third Dragon Secret: In the mysterious underground cave there are many doors, which include one secret passageway that leads to the cave of the dragons . . . but I can't tell you where it is, because I was blindfolded!

IN THE HEART
OF THE MOUNTAIN

The cave was totally **silent**. In fact, it was so quiet I could hear my own heartbeat!

BA-BUM BA-BUM BA-BUM BA-BUM

I was terrified!

Don't get me wrong. I like it when it's quiet. I love a quiet library. But a quiet cave can be a whole different story. What if there was a monster waiting for me by the exit?

"Get a grip, Geronimo," I told myself. I forced myself to look around. I saw **PreciOUS StOneS** embedded in the walls. They sparkled like stars. This part of the cave was very **HOT**. Maybe the dragon egg needed to be kept warm.

As for me, I was sweating my fur off!

First it had been chilly. Now it was SWELTERING. Someone could catch a really **bad cold** with all these temperature changes!

I kept walking until I spotted a large opening with daylight **shining** through. This had to be the exit that Pong had told me about. Cheese niblets! I was relieved. One more minute in that

eerily silent cave and they'd be locking me up in the Mad Mouse Center!

When I reached the opening, I saw that I would have to pass through three imposing metal gates. The first was made of **bronze**, the second was made of silver, and the third was made of gold.

Lucky for me, I didn't need a key or password to open the gates. They had already been broken into! The **bronze** one had been yanked back like it was made of **rubber**. Youch! Whoever did that must have really strong arms!

The silver one had a lock that was completely SCRATCHED up.

The scratches looked like giant claw marks!

BRONZE GATE

SILVER GATE

GOLDEN GATE

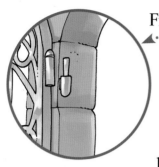

Finally, the **golden gate** was completely unhinged. Someone had lifted it off the wall. Whoever it was must have been incredibly powerful!

Then, right as I was leaving the cave, I found a piece of fancy **RED** fabric. Could it belong to whoever stole the **dragon's egg**?

I left the cave feeling like I was completely in the **DARK**. First, I still had no idea who the traitor was. And second, since I had promised Pong I'd put on the **BLINDFOLD** again, I couldn't see a thing!

WAA! WAA! WAA!

After my investigation of the cave, I was more confuſed than ever. I felt like I was forgetting something, but what?

I went to the library to think about things. When I got there, I wrote down all the strange things I had noticed.

1 To enter the cave you need to know the **SECRET PASSWORD**. (Only the most trusted of Sterling's colleagues know it.)

2 The bars on the bronze gate were **YANKED** open. (Only someone with really strong wrists could have done that.)

3 The lock on the silver gate was SCRATCHED. (The scratches look like giant claw marks.)

4 The golden gate was lifted from its hinges. (Only someone really powerful could have done that.)

5 Someone dressed in RED was in the cave. (Maybe the traitor wore a red outfit.)

I was still thinking about the cave when Firebreath III entered the library. He was sneezing so loudly I nearly fell off the bench I was sitting on. "**AAAACHOOO!**"

I wondered how he had gotten such a terrible cold.

I was about to ask when without warning he pulled out a tissue and began to sob hysterically.

"Waaaa! Waaaa! Waaa!" he cried. "What a tragedy! The dragon egg is lost forever!"

He **stomped** his feet, sending a few books tumbling off the shelves. Wow! What a drama king!

Even though tears were pouring out of Firebreath's eyes, I still got the feeling he wasn't being genuine.

He blew his nose loudly into his tissue. **Honk! Honk! Honk!**

Then he glanced back to make sure I was watching him. When he leaned closer, I gagged.

Eww…

His breath **reeked** of onions!

"Something wrong?" Firebreath asked.

I wanted to tell him he needed to brush his teeth, but I didn't want to be rude, so instead, I mumbled, "You must like **onions**!"

"I **HATE** them!" he replied. "But I love **spicy** peppers!"

Even just thinking about peppers made Firebreath **drool**. It was gross. But what happened next was even grosser.

Something **slimy** dropped from the dragon's tissue.

ONION TEARS

Why do onions make you cry? Because they contain amino acid sulfoxides. When you cut an onion, a sulfuric gas is released, which makes your eyes tear.

Onions also contain some medicinal qualities. Some studies have shown onions help in lowering cholesterol and reducing the length of the common cold.

Firebreath picked it up, but I had already seen what it was.

It was a piece of an onion!

I couldn't believe it! Firebreath had been using the onion to make his eyes tear up! I *knew* all that loud slobbery boo-hooing was way over the top!

Now I just had to figure out why. Why was Firebreath FAKING his crying?

I knew only one thing for sure: FIREBREATH couldn't be trusted!

LIES

It doesn't pay to tell lies, because they always have negative consequences!

If we tell lies, when the truth comes out, the person we lied to won't be able to trust us anymore. It's better to tell the truth and maintain the trust and respect of others.

???

WITCHES AND PRICKLY BUSHES

I spent the night tossing in bed. No, it wasn't because the dragons had stuck me in a room with **STONE** furniture again. In fact, my bed was **EXTRA-SOFT** and comfy. I just couldn't stop thinking about Firebreath's suspicious behavior.

Since I couldn't sleep, I was gazing up at the shining moon, when I felt a gust of **freezing cold** air. Suddenly, a **BLACK** figure appeared above the trees, blocking out the moonlight.

I recognized the

CACKLE

Cackle is the Queen of the Kingdom of Witches. She is the Never-named, the Black Queen, the Lady of Chills, the Empress of Nightmares, the Sorceress of Sorcerers, the Teacher of Spells, the Powerful Mistress, the Witchiest Witch, the Lady-General of the Dark Army, She Who Commands the Terror and Governs the Creatures of the Night.

shape immediately. It was Cackle, the Queen of the Witches.

"**OUCH!**" I shrieked. Without realizing it, I had twisted my tail into a knot.

I rushed out of the room, completely forgetting that dragon houses don't have stairs.

I **FELL** and landed in a **prickly** bush!

"**OUCH!**" I yelled again. Then I covered my mouth. If Cackle heard me,

I was in deep trouble.

Suddenly, I heard voices *whispering*.

The first voice was Cackle's.

"You did a fabuloussssss job and will sssssssooon

be repaid. Sssssterling will lose her kingdom in **sssssseven daysssss**!" she hissed.

A **DEEP** voice exclaimed, "And it will finally be mine! **All mine!**"

"Yes, but only if you complete your tasssk . . . ," Cackle warned.

"The **dragon egg** is hidden, Your Nastiness. When Sterling is gone, we will destroy her kingdom!" the **deep** voice said.

"And then all of the Kingdom of Fantasy will be in my power!" Cackle cried. But then she stopped.

"Tell me, do you **sssssmell** sssomething mousey around here?" she asked.

I didn't stay to hear the answer. I took off as fast as my paws could carry me. Let me tell you, it wasn't easy with all the armor I had on!

By the time I made it back to my room, I was beat. I fell asleep and dreamed of onions and witches and prickly bushes.

WE CAN DO IT!

At dawn, Pong woke me with a **grunt**.
"Sterling is waiting for you, Knight. The Great Council is meeting," he said.

So much for sleeping late! I moaned silently.

When I reached the **secret** meeting room, the other dragons were already waiting.

"So, Knight, have you discovered anything?" Sterling asked.

Once again, I felt like the bad-news mouse. But what could I do? I told Sterling how I had heard Cackle making a **pact** with the traitor who had stolen the **egg**.

The room erupted in **GROANS**.

"This is terrible news!" Sterling cried. "But

of course, only a witch would do something so despicable. Only she would steal the last precious **dragon egg**!"

All the dragons nodded in agreement. All of them except Firebreath.

He **rolled** his eyes at Sterling. "Forget the witch, Princess. It was your job to keep that **egg** safe and you blew it!" He smirked. "You have a **week** left to find that **egg**, or you're history!"

Sterling nodded. She wouldn't disobey the Dragon Laws. But there was still time left to find that **egg**.

"Knight, you must leave immediately to find the **egg**. Only you will be successful on this horrifyingly **DANGEROUS** mission!" she insisted.

I turned pale. Horrifyingly **DANGEROUS**? I almost fainted just thinking about it! But before I could explain that I was not the right mouse for the job, Sterling continued.

"Who wants to go with the knight on this **DANGEROUS** mission?" she asked.

At first no one said anything. Then a squawky voice said, "I will!" Scribblehopper popped up from under the table.

"You shouldn't be in here," Sterling said SOFTLY. "But you are a devoted friend to the knight. You may go with him!"

At this, Scribblehopper began LEAPING around the room happily and chattering away.

I wanted to protest. Scribblehopper is such a chatterbox he can drive a mouse up a clock! Still, no one else wanted to come along. Plus, when I thought about it, I realized Scribblehopper

> **FRIENDS ARE FABUMOUSE!**
>
> You can have lots of different types of friends. Some may be very talkative. Some may be quiet and shy. It doesn't matter if they are not exactly like you. What's important is that you care about each other!

really was a **GOOD** friend. He had **helped** me out before in the Kingdom of Fantasy. And this time I had a feeling I'd need all the help I could get!

We left right away. Sparkle and the *Dragon of the Rainbow* waited for us at the top of a hill.

At that moment, Sterling appeared.

"Knight, I didn't say it sooner because the

GREAT COUNCIL would have stopped me, but I will come with you, too," she said.

Next Sparkle bowed her head. "And I will follow you, courageous Sterling," she said.

Then, the Dragon of the Rainbow sang, "You can count on me! We can do it, you'll see!"

Now, I know it sounds sappy, but right then my heart filled with hope. All that positive thinking was making me a confident mouse. Maybe we could find the lost egg. Maybe we could save Sterling from banishment!

"We'll call ourselves the Company of the Silver Dragons!" I announced. "Let's go!"

I took one pawstep. Then I stopped. My whiskers drooped. "Uh, there's only one problem," I confessed. "I have no idea where we're going."

But just when I was feeling like a total failure, I spotted something overhead.

A **WHITE WINGED HORSE** with a scroll tied around its neck landed in front of us! Bowing its head, it said, "Knight, I have a **message** for you, from Blossom, the Queen of the Fairies."

I unrolled the scroll and read the message. It was written in the FANTASIAN ALPHABET.*

Are you able to translate it?

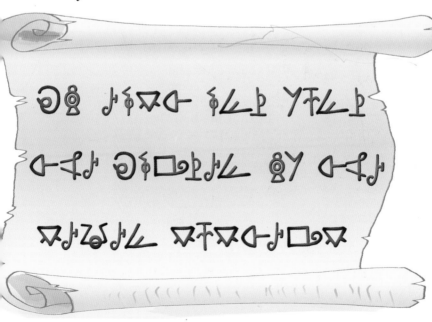

* You can find the Fantasian Alphabet on page 311.

I read the message aloud:

"'*Go east and find the Garden of the Seven Sisters.*'"

What GARDEN? What *sisters*?

I had no clue what the message meant. Still, I didn't want everyone to think I was a total **NINCOMPOOP** as a leader, so I said, "Um, we must go east. Let's fly toward the rising sun!"

FOLLOW THE SUN!

If you are lost and don't have a compass, all you need to do is look for the sun. The sun always rises in the east and always sets in the west.

In Search of
the Lost Egg

I Hate Flying!

I **CLIMBED** onto the back of the Dragon of the Rainbow with Scribblehopper right behind me. Sterling mounted Sparkle. Then we shot off into the rising pink dawn sky. I would tell you it was a beautiful sight, but I had my eyes **SQUEEZED** shut.

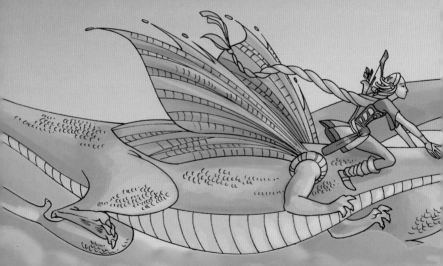

Oh, how I hate **taking** off . . . and **landing** . . . and, well, **everything** about flying!

When I fly on an airplane, I hate sitting by the window, because I'm afraid to look outside. But I also hate sitting on the aisle, because I'm afraid I'll get sick and the whole plane will see me!

Flying on a dragon is even worse. There are no windows and no **airsickness bags**! **Cheese niblets!** It's scary!

No sooner had we started flying than Scribblehopper began **chattering** away a mile a minute. I tried my best to block out his voice, but it was no use.

"Guess what, Sir Knight? The most amazing idea just flip-flopped into my head. You want to hear it? **Want to? Want to? Want to?**" he babbled.

Oh, how I wanted to **STUFF** a sock into his mouth. But instead, I said, "Okay."

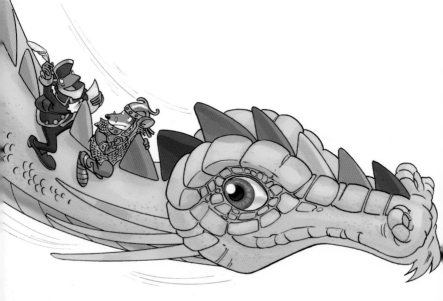

Scribblehopper then told me that he had decided to write a **long** poem for the dragons.

"I'll work on it as we fly," he **croaked**.

For the next couple of hours, he recited one bad line after the next. I wanted to **scream**.

To calm my nerves I tried concentrating on Blossom's mysterious message. I had so many questions. . . .

Who were the **SEVEN SISTERS**?

WHERE would I find them?

I was concentrating so hard I barely heard Scribblehopper's **voice** chattering away

Tap tap

behind me. But then I felt him **tap-tapping** on my armor.

"Want to hear my poem so far, Knight?" he babbled.

I **ignored** him. But then he yelled in my ear,

"KNIGHT!"

Kniiiiiiight!

I was so surprised I lost my balance!

I would have splattered on the ground if the Dragon of the Rainbow hadn't **grabbed** my tail!

I found myself hanging with my head down, suspended in midair!

Heelllp!

Cheesecake! Now I knew why I never went on those crazy rides at the Scampertown Carnival. Who would want to swing upside down by their tail on purpose?! I was so terrified I couldn't even **squeak**!

But then, as I stared in horror at the approaching ground below, the clouds parted and I saw an **INCREDIBLE** sight. It was a garden.

Could we be so lucky? Could it really be the **GARDEN OF THE SEVEN SISTERS**?

Geronimo Stilton

THE GARDEN OF THE SEVEN SISTERS

A few minutes later, we landed in front of a GLITTERING golden gate. Next to the gate was a GOLD PLAQUE with some writing on it. It was written using the FANTASIAN ALPHABET. Can you translate it?*

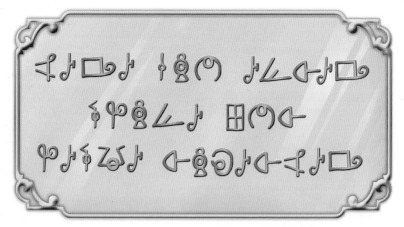

My head was still spinning from my upside-down ride, so Sterling read the words aloud:

* You can find the Fantasian Alphabet on page 311.

"*'Here you enter alone but leave together'*!"

What did that strange message mean?

I stared at the gate. It was **LOCKED** and could be opened only with a key.

I was trying to figure out where I might find the key when I heard a little voice calling me.

"Pssst! Psssst! Pssst!"

I looked around, but I didn't see anyone.

"Did anyone hear a little voice?" I asked.

My friends looked at me as if my cheese had **slipped** off my cracker.

Just then I heard the voice again.

"Hey, you! You with the funny armor!"

I blinked. I still couldn't see where the voice was coming from.

I started to **PANIC**. Maybe I really was

cracking up. I *was* hearing *little* voices. What next? Would I start singing nursery rhymes?

But right then I saw something. It was a spiderweb.

As I peered closer at the web, I spotted a tiny ladybug. The ladybug was waving at me frantically. She was trapped in the web.

Very carefully, I plucked the ladybug from the strands of the web. She was so happy she danced a little jig.

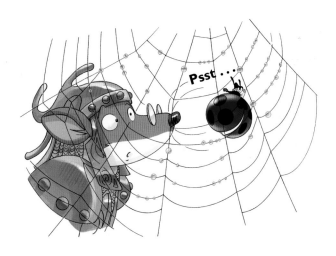

"Oh, **thank you**! You saved my life!" she exclaimed. "Another minute in that web and I would have been **lunch meat**. That spider has the **biggest** appetite ever. He's a nonstop **munching machine**! I mean, he should really learn how to pace himself. It's so unhealthy to eat like that."

The ladybug spoke so fast my head was **spinning**. I was going to respond but I couldn't get a word in.

"You must be the **TWELFTH KNIGHT**," she went on. "They said you'd be brave and kind. Oh, where are my manners? I forgot to introduce myself. My name is **Bitsy Luckybug**. And as you can see, I'm a pretty **LUCKY** bug! I am the Princess of the Kingdom of Greenfields." Suddenly, she frowned.

"Knight, I hate to be a **bother**, but can I come with you? I just know that spider is after me," she **cried**.

I told Bitsy we'd love to have her.

Bitsy **CLAPPED** her hands. Then she grew serious. "Now I must tell you some bad news," she said. "You have reached the **GARDEN OF THE SEVEN SISTERS**. Unfortunately, dragons are not allowed inside!"

We were all upset about separating from the dragons. But we had no choice.

Sterling told the dragons to leave but to return immediately when they heard the **sound** of her flute.

BITSY LUCKYBUG

BITSY LUCKYBUG

BITSY LUCKYBUG

THE PRINCESS OF THE
KINGDOM OF GREENFIELDS

itsy Luckybug is the Princess of the Kingdom of Greenfields. She is a small ladybug with a kind heart. Her palace lies within a poppy, and she is always happy. She has a tendency to speak very, very fast — so listen closely to her, or you might miss something! Bitsy appreciates beauty even in the small things around her. She considers herself incredibly lucky and has the ability to pass on her lucky feeling to others.

Bitsy is very smart and speaks many bug languages, including cicadese, antese, grasshoppish, roachen, and wormish. Even though she is small, she is very brave. There is only one thing that fills her heart with dread: spiders! Spiders work for the evil Cackle, and for quite some time they have been a threat to the ladybug population.

The minute the dragons left, I began to worry. What if one of Cackle's GIGANTIC spiders came after us while we were inside the garden? How would we be able to get away? I wasn't exactly FAST on my paws. In grade school, I always finished dead last when we ran the half mile on field day.

Now I took a LONG, deep breath and stared at the locked golden gate. I still had no idea how we were going to get inside.

"Do we say a magic word?" Scribblehopper asked Bitsy.

"Oh, no." The ladybug giggled. "To enter you just need to have a PURE HEART and ask nicely."

It seemed a strange way to open the gate, but I had no other ideas, so I knocked.

"May I please enter?" I said, feeling foolish. After all, who talks to a gate?

But as soon as I finished speaking, the gate opened with a loud creak.

CRREEEEAAAAAAAAAK!

SPRING!

As we entered the garden, a **SCARY** thought occurred to me. Was it easy to get into the garden only because it was hard to get **OUT**?

My paws immediately felt like ten-ton weights. I was paralyzed with fear!

Snap out of it, Geronimo, I scolded myself.

I was here to help Sterling, not to be a 'fraidy mouse. There wasn't time for a nervous breakdown!

I took a **DEEP BREATH** and looked around the garden. It was all very **beautiful**. A warm wind ruffled my fur and the scent of flowers filled the air.

We were surrounded by fields of lush **GREEN** grass and cherry trees in full bloom.

On the branches of the trees, the birds were chirping, and the flower beds were filled with deep **RED** roses, **yellow** tulips, and pretty daisies.

Even though the garden was beautiful, there was something strange about it. Then it hit me. It was SPRING!

This was strange, because a few feet away, right outside the gate . . . it was FALL!

How was that possible?

SOMEONE IS
WATCHING US

"Something odd is going on here," I said. "How come it's **SPRING** in here and **FALL** out there?" I pointed back toward the gate.

We all agreed it was **strange**.

Then, Sterling grew still. "Everyone, please be Quiet," she whispered. "Someone is watching us."

I whirled around. I didn't see anyone. "Where?" I asked.

"Yeah, where?" Scribblehopper croaked.

"I can't see them, but I **sense** their presence," Sterling explained.

At that moment I thought I heard laughter.

"Ha! Ha! Ha!   Hee! Hee! Hee!"

It was coming from the tree branches above us.
Just then a strong, **flowery-scented** gust
of wind surrounded us, causing . . .

. . . my helmet to **faLL** off my head . . .

. . . Sterling's braid
to unravel . . .

. . . Scribblehopper's hat to take **flight** . . .

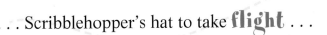

. . . and Bitsy to **cLIng**
to my sleeve for dear life!

Aaachoo!

Plus, with all the pollen in the air, I
couldn't stop **snEEzIng**.

A moment later, surrounded by a cloud of SCENTED petals, two **graceful** creatures appeared.

One had wild blonde hair and the other had long hair filled with flowers. They both bowed.

"My name is **Breeze**, the nymph of the wind, and this is Primrose, the nymph of the flowers," the one with the blonde hair said. "We are the youngest of the **SEVEN SISTERS**.

Welcome to our garden!"

Breeze grinned at me impishly. Then she blew a

Primrose & Breeze

Primrose and Breeze are the nymphs that make the spring season burst into bloom. Primrose is sweet and makes the flowers blossom. Breeze is spunky and brings the spring wind.

gust of wind that **ruffled** my fur.

"Knight, the spring wind has brought me news of your **problems**. I know that you are on a **DANGEROUS** mission. I know that the Princess of the Silver Dragons has been betrayed and that the dragon egg has been **STOLEN**," she said.

Next Primrose smiled at me and I was overcome with the scent of flowers. "**Aaachoo!**" I sneezed right in her face. How **embarrassing**!

She politely pretended not to notice, then said, "Knight, I know that you are in need of help. We would like to give you some **gifts** and some **precious** advice. But . . ." Her voice trailed off.

I stared at her **anxiously**, waiting for her to continue.

"But?" I coaxed.

"But . . . ," she replied slowly.

But whaaaat?! I screamed inside my head. **BUT** she wasn't going to give me the gifts because she didn't like my fur? BUT she wanted to eat lunch first? BUT Santa Mouse was coming to town?!

Finally, when I thought I would explode with curiosity, she said, "But . . . before you can go on your way to the next part of the garden, you need to pass a tiny little TEST. Who would like to volunteer?"

Everyone else took a step backward . . . so it looked like I had volunteered!

I started to sweat.

The two nymphs looked nice enough, but what if this was all one big trick?

A FLOWER AND A BUTTERFLY

Before putting me to the test, Breeze gave me a LITTLE BUTTERFLY carved from a precious light blue stone. "Here is my gift," she said. "When you are in **TROUBLE**, and you don't know where to go, it will remind you to try to see things from different points of view — as if you had WINGS!"

Then Primrose handed me a rosebud.

"This gift is given to you with KINDNESS," she said. If you, too, give it to someone with KINDNESS . . . you will get a special surprise."

I thanked them for the

THE SECRET OF THE BUTTERFLY

The butterfly is fragile and weak, but . . . it knows how to fly. It can leave the ground and see everything from above. This is its secret: Because it can see from other points of view, it can better understand itself and others.

gifts, even though I didn't really understand how I would use them. I mean, call me crazy, but how could a flower and a butterfly help me find the dragon egg? I was hoping for a clue, a map, or maybe even a grilled cheese sandwich. I had missed lunch and my stomach was rumbling!

I guess Breeze could see the disappointment on my face, because she said, "Never fear, Knight. In time you will understand the WORTH of our gifts. Blossom told us to save them for you."

I put the gifts into my bag and took a step. But before I got anywhere, Breeze crept up behind me and blindfolded me!

"Oh, no, Knight!" She giggled. "Don't you remember? If you want to continue on your way, you need to pass a tiny little test. . . ."

THE MYSTERIOUS
SCENT . . .

I was trying not to panic when Primrose held something under my nose.

"Knight, you will now smell a **mysterious** scent. If you don't guess what it is . . . you must stay here **FOREVER**!" she said.

So much for not panicking! We had only **seven** days to find the dragon egg. I couldn't

It smelled like . . . it smelled like . . .

be in the garden **FOREVER**!

Cautiously, I began to sniff.

I SNIFFED . . . and I SNIFFED . . . and I SNIFFED! It was a **Sweet**, *flowery* scent. In fact, it was so sweet I was beginning to feel nauseous.

I gulped for air.

My nose became swollen and **RED** from so much sniffing. Then I began to sneeze.

"Aaaachoo! Aaaachoo! Aaaachoo!"

"Well, Knight? Do you know what it is?" Primrose asked.

By now my head was **pounding**, my nose was running, and my stomach was **CHURNING**. But what could I do? I had to say something.

Meanwhile, the nymphs had begun to sing. . . .

"TAKE A GUESS.
HERE'S A CLUE:
THIS SCENT IS NAMED AFTER
A RAINBOW HUE!"

My mind raced. What smelled sweet and was named after a color of the rainbow? Red, orange, yellow, green, blue, indigo, and . . . Suddenly, I knew the answer. "Violet!" I yelled.

I threw the blindfold off. I was right! My friends were so happy they cheered!

Good job!   Hooray for the knight!

Yippee!

SPRING

Summer

SUMMER!

We said good-bye to Breeze and Primrose and continued on our way. Immediately, we realized something strange had happened. It was suddenly much **HOTTER**. The `cicadas` hummed, the bees fluttered around, the colors of the flowers were richer, and the grass was a darker shade of GREEN. It was summer!

Scribblehopper began to HOP around.

"Look at all these **COLORS**. I'm so inspired! I've got to write another poem!" he declared.

Oh, no. Not more **bad** poetry! I winced. "We don't have time. We've got to figure out how to get out of here," I told the frog.

Just then Bitsy flew onto my shoulder. "Leave it to me, Knight," she said. "I'll go ask those cicadas. I speak their language."

Bitsy took off and landed by a group of cicadas. They appeared to be having a concert on a patch of **POPPIES**. When Bitsy arrived, they stopped PLAYING their instruments and began chattering away a mile a minute.

CLICK CLICK CLICK!

"What did they say?" I asked after Bitsy returned.

Summer Summer

"It's easy to get out!" she said. "We just have to go that way, then a bit that way, then to the **right**, then to the **left**, and then to the **right** again. . . ."

We followed her directions but ended up wandering around and around for hours in the **blazing** sun. **Holey cheese!** We were lost!

Finally, we decided to rest under the shade of a large peach tree.

But suddenly, the tree we were leaning on **disappeared**!

In its place, **two** maidens appeared. One had an **olive** branch and the other had a basket of **ʃeedʃ**.

"I am Peachflower, the nymph of fruit, and this is my sister Seedling, the nymph of the earth," said one of the maidens. "We are two of the Seven Sisters. Blossom sent us to help you."

She handed me an **olive** branch.

Then she said, "When everything seems to be going poorly, and

THE OLIVE

The olive has been an important symbol throughout history. The ancient Greeks used an olive wreath as a symbol of victory, and the ancient Romans saw the olive as a symbol of the goddess of peace (Pax).

Peachflower & Seedling

These two sisters are the nymphs of the summer. They work together closely to make sure plants thrive and produce vibrant and delicious fruits.

war seems inevitable, this olive branch will remind you that the most precious thing is *peace*."

Next Seedling stepped forward. She gave me a handful of golden seeds. "From these *tiny* seeds, **BiG** things will grow, just as a *tiny* hidden seed under the earth grows to be a **BiG** plant filled with fruit."

I *thanked* the sisters even though I had no idea what I would do with an old branch and some seeds. Then I asked them if they could give us directions.

"Cross that bridge and pass that tall hedge. There you will find the path to the next part of the garden," Seedling instructed.

Soon we passed under a *flowered* archway.

AUTUMN!

It didn't take us long to realize we were again entering a new season. The leaves on the trees were now YELLOW, RED, and **bROWN**. There was a chill in the air. It was autumn!

Suddenly, two winged nymphs appeared before us.

I let out a squeak. **Cheese niblets!** These sisters kept POPPING up everywhere!

Hourly & Crystal

Hourly and Crystal are the autumn nymphs. Hourly is the nymph of time. She marks the passing of hours by turning a large golden hourglass. Crystal is the nymph of clear water and represents purity and sincerity.

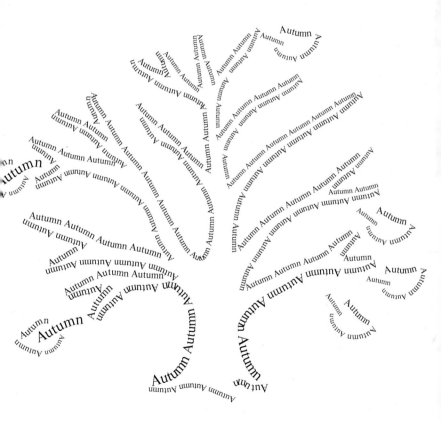

One of them shook her head quickly back and forth. "Knight, you're **LATE**! You need to get moving! How do you expect to find that **dragon egg** at the rate you're going?" she scolded.

"We got lost . . . ," I began. But the nymph cut me off.

"No **time** for excuses. Believe me! I am **HOURLY**, the nymph of **time**, and I know a thing or two about it. So I'll be quick. I am giving you this **golden hourglass** as a gift. Just **squeeze** this button and it will make the sand stop running. Then, for a whole hour, **time** will stop."

I grinned. Now this was a gift I could use! For example, I could use it to give myself an **EXTRA**

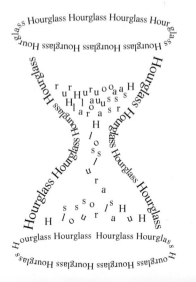

TIME IS PRECIOUS

Time is always going by. Use each second wisely, because every instant is unique. If you want to give someone a truly special gift, offer the most precious thing you have: your time!

hour in the morning. I hate getting out of my cozy, warm bed. Or I could use it when I was late to meet my grandfather. He gets furious when that happens.

I was still thinking about the hourglass when the other nymph stepped forward. Her long GReen hair was sopping wet.

"I am Crystal, the nymph of WATER," she said. Then she handed me a crystal vial. "This is the water of life. It comes from the fountain of youth. Just one drop can heal wounds, one sip gives strength, and two sips bring youth. But be careful — no one should ever drink more than two sips," she explained.

Thanking the sisters, we continued on our way.

Autumn

WINTER

THE GIFT OF SILENCE!

After a short while, the weather changed once more. This time, thick snowflakes *whirled* around us, pushed by the **freezing** wind. Icicles clung to my whiskers. Frozen feta! It was WINTER!

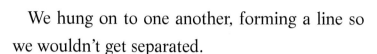

We hung on to one another, forming a line so we wouldn't get separated.

The **snowstorm** carried us straight to a **frozen** lake. At its center, I noticed a mysterious figure.

It looked like an **ICE** statue wrapped in a cloak.

When we got closer, I noticed that at the foot of the statue there was a sign made of **ICE**. It said: **My name is Arctica. My gift is silence**.

Silence? What was that supposed to mean?

I was so confused I just stared at the statue in silence. I wondered where we should go next. **Where? Where? Where?**

SILENCE IS GOLDEN

When we need to do something important, like thinking about a big decision, doing our homework, or getting a good night's sleep, we usually look for a quiet place. Silence helps us concentrate without distractions. This is the meaning behind the saying "Silence is golden"!

Arctica

Arctica, the seventh sister, is the nymph of winter and of snow. She lives alone in her part of the garden because she loves silence. She wears a dress of ice and a crown of snowflakes. She spends her time decorating the garden with delicate lace made of frost.

Just as I was beginning to feel like a **Frozen** failure, I noticed something about the statue. She was **pointing** toward a spot on the horizon, as if she wanted to show us the way.

My heart **skipped** a beat. Could it be? It seemed like she was telling us to continue toward a far-off mountain!

Right at that moment on the **SIGN** at her feet, a new message appeared:

Well done, Knight! Good luck!

Yes! I was so excited I **jumped** into the air, slipped on a patch of ice, and **tumbled** into a mound of snow. Did I mention I'm a little bit of a klutz?

My friends helped me up, and I thanked Arctica for her help **silently** by writing her a message in the snow: **THANK YOU!**

Then we continued on.

We walked all day through the **wintery** garden. As we walked, I thought about the gifts I'd received. A handful of seeds . . . a vial of water. . . . They were all so strange. I wished I knew what I was supposed to do with them, but my brain was so **FROZEN** I could hardly think!

Finally, in the middle of the night, we arrived at the golden gate. Back where we started . . .

back where we started! . . . back where we started . . .

THE GIFTS OF THE SEVEN SISTERS

From the nymphs of spring, Geronimo received a stone butterfly and a rosebud. From the summer nymphs, he received seeds and an olive branch. From the autumn nymphs, he received an hourglass and a vial of the water of life. From the nymph of winter, he received the gift of silence.

THE LABORS OF
THE KNIGHT

BADA-BAAANG!

The **golden gate** in front of us was locked again.

As I looked up at it, Scribblehopper urged, "Not to be a **pain**, Sir Knight, but can you hurry it up? We're **freezing**! Ask the gate to open!"

No problem! I thought. All I had to do was ask nicely. So I said, "Can we **please** leave?"

Nothing happened.

"Oh, Mr. Gate, will you **please** open up?" I asked again.

Still **nothing**.

"Pretty **please** with a **cherry** on top?" I tried, feeling desperate.

Nothing.

I couldn't take it anymore. I grabbed the bars and shook them. When they didn't budge, I

KICKED my feet, **rolled** on the ground, **pulled** my whiskers, and, finally, took off my glasses so I could sob freely. It was so **cold** my tears froze on my fur! Rats!

Still the gate remained locked. In fact, I thought I even heard it chuckling. "Tee hee hee . . ."

But that must have been my imagination.

Then I remembered the **ENGRAVING** at the entrance. It said:

HERE YOU ENTER ALONE
BUT LEAVE TOGETHER.

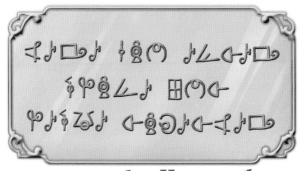

Right then I got a **brilliant idea**.

"Let's all hold hands. If we try to leave together,

maybe the gate will open," I suggested. "On three . . . two . . . one!"

BADA-BAAAANG!

We ran into the closed gate with a **bang**! So much for my brilliant idea.

At this point, I was dying to sit down and start crying again, but I did my best to control myself. Partly because I didn't want the others to think I was a **wimp** and partly because I didn't really want to sit in the snow. My tail would **freeze**!

I stared at the gate, thinking. It was very tall and would be **dangerous** to climb.

Then Bitsy said, "I could pass through the bars. Would that help?"

I jumped up. "It could help if we had a **rope**! You could **fly** past the gate, tie the rope to a high-up tree branch, and then we could use it to **climb** out! Now we just need a rope."

Sterling rose to her feet without saying a word.

She undid her braid and with a **WHACK** of her sword, she chopped off a lock of her long hair.

"Here is our *rope*!" she said, smiling.

I was shocked. She gave us a piece of her beautiful hair! But this was an EMERGENCY and we needed to get to work.

We spent the rest of the night braiding Sterling's golden hair into a thick *rope*.

NO, YOU GO!

By the first light of **DAWN**, we had a long, braided rope of hair. It was fine, but sturdy, and gleamed in the sun. The wind had calmed down, and the sun shined **brightly**, lighting up the garden. Too bad it was as **cold** as the ice rink at Rockrat Center in the wintertime. **Brrr!**

Still, there was no time to worry about the weather. I set Bitsy on my paw and she prepared to take off. She grabbed the rope with her **TINY** paws and began to flap her **TINY** wings. Faster

and faster she flapped as the rest of us cheered her on encouragingly.

"Come on, you can do it!" "Fly, Bitsy, fly!"

Slowly, Bitsy lifted off into the air. She looked just like a tiny HELICOPTER, dragging the long golden rope behind her.

After what seemed like forever, the ladybug arrived at the first THICK branch and flew around it several times, making a sort of figure eight.

Then she flew back toward us, **TUGGING** at the rope.

She had done it! She had tied a knot!

We all yelled, "Hooray! Three cheers for Bitsy!"

But then Bitsy was so exhausted she began to fall. . . .

In a *flash*, Scribblehopper h o p p e d up and grabbed her before she splattered onto the ground! We all crowded around him, staring at Bitsy, whose eyes were closed.

"Oh, no! Is she okay?" Scribblehopper *croaked*.

Sterling gently touched the ladybug's wing. "She's **FAINTED**, but I think she'll be okay. She's just cold and extremely tired."

At this, Scribblehopper **ripped** a cuff from his jacket and wrapped it around Bitsy like a warm blanket.

At that moment, Bitsy opened her eyes. She stared up at Scribblehopper and said, "**My hero!** You saved my life! I'll never forget it!"

Scribblehopper **puffed** up his chest with pride. "Not a big deal," he croaked. "Although, that was a pretty good catch. Maybe I should write a long, long **poem** about it. . . ."

Meanwhile, Sterling had *GRABBED* hold of the rope.

"Hurry!" she called. "We have to go before another **blizzard** starts. I'll CLIMB first, then everyone follow me one by one!"

My paws began to **shake**. I didn't want

to climb. I'm afraid of heights! I tried to get Scribblehopper to go before me.

"Here, my froggy friend, you go ahead," I suggested.

"No, **YOU** go," he replied.

"No, **YOU**," I insisted.

"No, **YOU**," he said.

Sterling NARROWED her eyes.

"Come on!" she ordered.

So I took a deep breath and began to climb up the tree.

Oh, how I hate climbing! Even as a young mouselet I never liked to **CLIMB** the mousey bars. Why do they have to build them so **far** off the ground, anyway?

I was starting to feel **dizzy**, but I had to keep going. Another snowstorm was coming, and I didn't want to be FROZEN alive! I chewed my whiskers as I put paw over paw over paw. . . .

Before I knew it, I had done it!

WHY HADN'T I THOUGHT OF THAT BEFORE?

I was so **happy** to have reached the top I accidentally let go of the tree branch and almost PLUNGED to the ground! Luckily, Sterling grabbed my paw right at the last minute. **Whew!**

Eventually, we each made it out of there in one piece. Now I knew why the sign said **HERE YOU ENTER ALONE BUT LEAVE TOGETHER!** If we hadn't all worked together, we'd be stuck in that crazy garden **FOREVER**!

I was still thinking about the GARDEN as we headed into the morning sun. We were back in autumn in this part of the kingdom, and the leaves **CRUNCHED** beneath my paws. I was thrilled to be out of the garden and felt full of

energy. I led the group down a *winding* path, squeaking, "When you're happy and you know it, clap your paws!"

But after a while, I noticed everyone else seemed to be **lagging** behind. When I turned around, Scribblehopper said, "Um, where are we going?"

"Any idea?" Sterling added.

"A clue?" Bitsy murmured.

I stopped **dead** in my tracks. Suddenly, I wasn't feeling so **energetic** anymore. In

fact, I felt completely exhausted. My head began to pound and a wave of panic swept over me.

Sour Swiss slices! I had no idea where we were or where we were headed!

"I don't know where we're going," I confessed. But then, not wanting to look like the WORST leader in the world, I quickly suggested, "How about we rest under this TREE and have a snack?"

I didn't know about the others, but I always think better on a full stomach. In fact, if I ate two large CHEESE PIZZAS and a mozzarella milkshake, I could probably find the lost dragon egg, restore the spring, and even end world hunger! Well, okay, maybe I couldn't end hunger, but you get the idea.

I nibbled on a piece of cheese and thought and thought and thought. . . .

Why had Blossom sent me

to the garden? Was it to get the **gifts** from the sisters? I pulled out the **blue stone butterfly**. It was supposed to teach you to look from other points of view.

What point of view did a butterfly have? It **FLEW**, so it could see things from above. . . .

I ʃmacked my forehead. That was it! Why hadn't I thought of that before?

I **JUMPED** to my paws. "I've got an idea!" I squeaked. "Let's *climb* that mountain over there. From there we can see things from above. We can get a better idea where we are and maybe we can find some clues to follow to the **dragon's egg**."

Sterling **JUMPED** up and stood next to me. "Great idea, Knight! Let's go!" she exclaimed.

Scribblehopper and Bitsy were less excited.

"Are you sure you want to climb that huge mountain right now?" Scribblehopper whined.

"I'd go," Bitsy added. "But I'm so **tired**. I don't know if I can make it."

In the end, Scribblehopper let Bitsy climb up onto his hat and we began walking. It was a **LONG** and tiresome journey. We passed through forests and fields and then up the **steep, ROCKY** mountain.

By the time we reached the top, it was already sunset. Looking out over the landscape, I spotted something **SPARKLING** far off on the horizon. I realized I was staring at the **CRYSTAL CASTLE**, Blossom's palace!

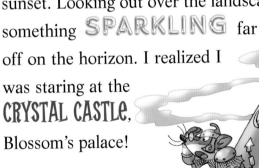

WHAT IS THAT SMELL?

Now I knew where we were. We had reached the border of the **Kingdom of Fairies**. Still, even though I now knew where we were, I had no idea where we should go.

Soon the sun disappeared from sight. Oh, how I hate the **DARK**, and black cats, and the Hungry Rodent **Cheese Shop** during the holidays. Have you ever been there? The crowds are unbelievable!

Anyway, where was I? . . . Oh, yes. It was **DARK**, so I decided that we should stay put and figure out what to do in the morning. After a quick snack, everyone fell right to sleep — except me.

I **tossed** and **TURNED** all night. At one

point, I thought I heard the wings of an enormouse **DRAGON** flying over me . . . but I must have been dreaming.

When I woke up, it was dawn. I stood up to **stretch** my paws and took a deep breath, filling my lungs with **FRESH** air. There was only one problem. The air wasn't fresh! It smelled like a **stinky** outhouse!

Right then, everyone else woke up, too.

"What is that horrible smell?" the princess cried.

"It's burning my eyes!" wailed Bitsy.

"SOMEBODY CATCH ME — I'M GOING TO PASS OUT" Scribblehopper croaked.

A DRAGON'S
LITTLE GIFT

I scratched my head, trying to figure out what was going on. The Kingdom of Fairies was known for its **rosy scent**. And let me tell you, this **STENCH** wasn't rosy. It was just plain **gross**.

I was still trying to identify the smell when suddenly Scribblehopper began hopping **up** and **down**. He was pointing to a strange **brown** hill in a grassy area nearby.

"What is that?" he said.

We went **down** to check it out. As we got closer, we realized the **smell** was coming from the hill. It **smelLed** awful!

I was ready to tuck in my tail and take off, but Sterling stopped me. It was then that I noticed the princess was **grinning**.

"This is great! We found a dragon clue, Knight!" she exclaimed.

I had no idea what the princess was talking about. In fact, I was beginning to think maybe the **stench** had gone to her head!

"CLUE?" I muttered, trying my best not to breathe through my nose.

The princess smiled. "Oh, Knight, don't you remember all the things I taught you about dragons?" she asked.

I have to admit I could barely remember my own name at that point. The **smell** was enough to kill me! But I didn't want to disappoint the princess, so I carefully searched the ground for **DRAGON PRINTS**.

Finally, I gave up. "Sorry, Princess, but I just don't see any **DRAGON CLUE** here," I said.

Sterling pointed to the brown hill. "Knight, *this* is the clue. It's a dragon's LiTTLe giFT," she

said with a wink.

Little gift? I thought, feeling even more confused. Then all of sudden it hit me. Little gift was another way to say dung! I was staring at large smelly DRAGON DROPPINGS!

"Okay, I get it, Princess. Now let's get out of here!" I squeaked, my stomach CHURNING.

But Sterling wouldn't budge.

"Oh, no, Knight, we can't go now," she said. "It is very strange to see dragon traces in this part of the kingdom. Before we can leave, we need to STUDY this well, to figure out when the DRAGON was here. This dragon might know something about the stolen **egg**!"

Now I really felt **sick** to my stomach. Oh, how had I gotten myself into such a *stinky* situation?

In a panic, I tried *running* away, but Sterling grabbed me by the tail.

"Don't worry, Knight. All you have to do is **EXAMINE** the droppings. If they're fresh, then we know the **DRAGON** was here recently."

I groaned. I was an author, not a **dung examiner**! But everyone was counting on me. So I held my nose and moved closer to the **stinky** brown mound. Once I was next to it, I could tell that it was very *fresh*.

"Good work!" the princess yelled.

But I didn't hear her.

I HAD ALREADY FAINTED FROM THE STENCH!

A STRANGE
PILE OF SEEDS

When I came to, I realized that I had accidentally **stepped** on the edge of the dragon droppings. **How disgusting!** I sprinted away from the **stinky** pile as fast as my paws could carry me, and jumped into a nearby brook, still wearing all my armor. My paw **stunk** so badly that even the fish swam away from me!

Even though I was in the brook, I was still feeling stinky. I swam over to a waterfall and let the **freezing** cold water sink into my fur. **Cheese niblets**, it was cold!

When I got out, I sat down in a patch of sun to dry myself off. It was **WARM** and cozy. Within minutes I was snoring away. **ZZZZZZZ!**

I dreamed I was eating a cheese Danish **HOT** out of the oven. When I woke up, I was drooling. How humiliating!

Then I saw something on the other side of the brook. A **clue**!

The clue was more dragon

What's this?

dung. This time I didn't even have to get really close to know it was fresh. **Pee-yoo!** The **smell** was worse than a sewer rat's **gym locker**!

A few minutes later, I noticed that even closer to me there was a **strange** pile of seeds and **RED** skins. I took off my glasses to clean them and almost fell right into the pile! When I put them back on, I realized the small mountain was made from the remains of a huge pile of **hot red peppers**. Who likes **RED** peppers? Dragons do! I had found another **CLUE**.

At that moment, my eyes began to burn from being near the peppers. Tears rolled down my fur and I began to sneeze like crazy. "**Aaachooo!**"

Aaachooo!

Oh, poor me! My nose felt like it was on FIRE, and I couldn't stop sneezing.

"Hurry, Knight, jump in the water!" Sterling said.

So I did. Unfortunately, the sun still hadn't warmed up the brook. It was still **freezing**. I shivered. **Cheese niblets!** I hoped this jumping-into-the-brook thing wasn't going to become a permanent habit.

Just then Bitsy flew over, *waving* excitedly. "Knight, guess what?!" she cried. "I found another LiTTLe giFT! Come check it out!"

Oh, no! Not another LiTTLe giFT! With a groan, I sank under the water. . . .

Blub. . . Blub. . . Blub. . .

CALL THE DRAGONS!

Eventually, I had to come up for air. After all, I'm a mouse, not a fish. I climbed out of the freezing brook, my teeth chattering. Then I headed back to the SUNNY patch of grass to dry off. I was beginning to feel like I was stuck in the middle of a HORRIBLE movie in which the day kept repeating itself over and over.

"CHEER UP, Knight." Sterling's voice broke into my thoughts. "You don't have to examine any more evidence. It's clear that the DRAGON passed through here not long ago. Maybe just before dawn."

I shivered again and this time it wasn't from the cold water. That meant I hadn't been DREAMING when I'd thought I'd heard a dragon the night before. It really had been there!

I decided we'd better get going. Time was running out and we needed to find that **dragon egg**. Too bad it was taking us so **long** to travel through the kingdom. Where was a good TAXICAB when you needed one?

At that moment Bitsy flew over my head, and I watched as she *zigzagged* quickly between the trees. Suddenly, I was hit with a fabumouse idea. Why hadn't I thought of it earlier?

"Sterling, quick, call the dragons! Then we can really move!" I said.

The princess played her SILVER FLUTE and within minutes the dragons arrived. We climbed aboard Sparkle and the *Dragon of the Rainbow* and took off in search of more dragon traces.

DRAGON TRACES

We found lots of **CLUES**, and they all seemed to come from a **DRAGON OF FIRE**:

1 First, the soft grass in the field was all torn up, as if someone had **landed HEAVILY** on the ground.

2 Second, the water in a nearby lake was muddy and **CHURNED** up, as if an **enormouse** creature had splashed around in it.

3 Third, there were many tree trunks that were burnt and **BLACKENED** from smoke. The damage could have been made by a dragon who couldn't

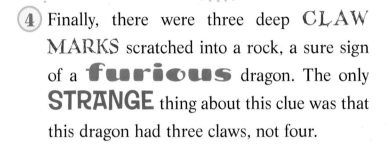

control his FIRE — such as one who was sneezing because of a really bad cold.

4 Finally, there were three deep CLAW MARKS scratched into a rock, a sure sign of a **furious** dragon. The only STRANGE thing about this clue was that this dragon had three claws, not four.

I had seen similar scratches before, but where? That evening, I RACKED my brain, trying to remember.

All that thinking made me sleepy. Before I knew it, I fell into a deep sleep...

WHAT A NIGHTMARISH NIGHT!

I dreamed that I was being chased by fire-breathing dragons with sharp claws and red eyes.

One dragon stood out from the pack. It was Firebreath III. He grabbed me and whispered menacingly,

"YOU WILL PAY FOR THISSSSSS!"

Suddenly, I understood everything.

I woke up squeaking, "**Help!!!!**"

Immediately, Sterling appeared at my side with

her **sword** drawn.

"What happened, Knight? Who is threatening you? I'll get them! Just point me in the right direction!" she cried. Did I mention the princess loves to do battle?

"Well, um, no, you see, they're not here. It was a **nightmare** with Firebreath III, and the SCRATCHES—I mean, the bad **cold**—I mean, the onion **smell** and the broken nail—I mean, the sprained paw and the **hot pepper seeds** . . . ," I babbled.

Sterling held up her hand. "It's okay, Knight, just try to calm down and start from the beginning," she urged me.

So I took a deep breath and SPILLED out the whole story. It had taken me a while, but I had finally figured out that the dragon we were tracking was also the one who had stolen the **dragon egg**.

1 The scratches on the rock were missing a claw mark, like the ones I had seen in the cave. Firebreath III had a broken claw.

2 I'd found a piece of red cloth on the heavy, unhinged gate in the cave. Firebreath III had a sprained wrist—possibly from breaking the gate—and was always dressed in red.

3 The dragon we were following loved to eat red peppers and had a cold . . . just like Firebreath III.

4 I saw Firebreath III sniffing an onion to make himself cry. He was only pretending to be upset over the stolen egg!

And after going back over all the clues, I realized that dragon was none other than the nasty-tempered King of the Dragons of Fire, FIREBREATH III!

Now the only thing I had to figure out was why FIREBREATH had stolen the egg.

The next morning, we got back on the road, following the DRAGON tracks. At least now we knew who we were chasing.

It wasn't long before we realized we were entering a new area: the Land of the Trolls.

TROLLS

Trolls are brutal creatures who hardly ever wash and have disgusting habits. They live underground in dirty, dark caves. They stink so badly you can smell them from miles away. When they go to battle, they bang their drums. Drum-de-drum-drum . . . drum-de-drum-drum.

In the Land
of the Trolls

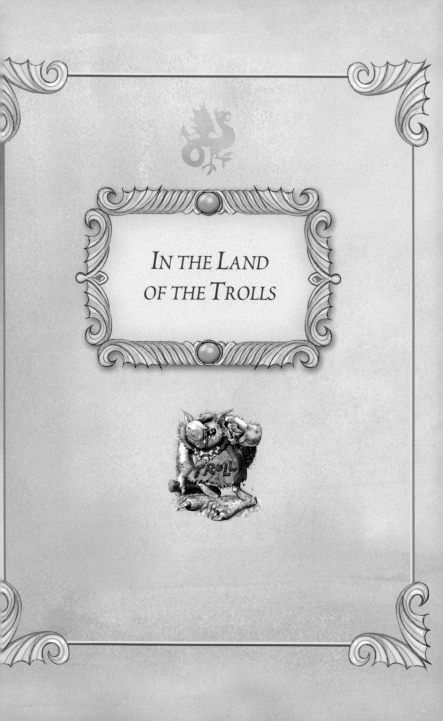

RUN!

As soon as we got near the Tribe of the Trolls, my heart began **beating** out of my fur. I remembered the **evil** creatures from my previous visits to the Kingdom of Fantasy. Let me just say I'd rather stick my tail in a blender than meet up with a troll!

I took a deep breath and tried to remain calm. It didn't work. Then I remembered I had the **BRAND OF LIGHT**. If danger was nearby, it would warn us with a blue light.

Slowly, I looked down at my paw. Holey cheese! It was lit up like a **Christmouse tree**!

"*RUN!*" I shrieked.

Suddenly, we heard the trolls' drums.

DRUM-DE-DRUM-DRUM ... DRUM-DE-DRUM-DRUM.
DRUM-DE-DRUM-DRUM ... DRUM-DE-DRUM-DRUM.
DRUM-DE-DRUM-DRUM ...

Soon, from the top of a tall cliff, the trolls began to throw **enormouse** rocks at us. Then they bombarded us with **deadly spears** and **ARROWS**.

They were aiming at the dragons' wings, trying to make us fall. If they caught us, they would turn us into **troll hamburgers**!

They yelled:

"Get them! Crush them!"
"Eat them! Mush them!"

I closed my eyes and tried to think of a plan. Oh, how had I gotten myself into such a mess? I was a good mouse. I never ran with scissors. I

Bitsy hid in Scribblehopper's hat!

ate all my fruits and vegetables. Well, except for **BRUSSELS SPROUTS**. I'm not crazy about them.

I was still thinking about vegetables when the *Dragon of the Rainbow* was hit. He began wobbling beneath me.

Suddenly, I knew what I had to do. I yelled to Sterling, "Princess! We'll stay here, and you steer the dragons away. If the **TROLLS** see them fly off, they will think we have all left. Then Scribblehopper, Bitsy, and I will **sneak** in."

SSSSSSHHH!

Sterling wasn't too happy about leaving us, but I told her it was our only choice. Once we lost the **trolls**, the rest of us could keep going. It was our only hope of finishing our **miſſion** and recovering the lost **dragon egg**. It was our only chance to save the dragon species.

A little while later, the *Dragon of the Rainbow* set us down on the top of a hill that was covered in troll **garbage**. Someone really needed to give that bunch a lesson on littering. **What a dump!**

Sterling said good-bye **reluctantly** and mounted Sparkle. Before she left, I told her, "If we don't make it back in three days, send someone out to look for us."

Oh, how I hoped we'd make it back **alive**!

The *Dragon of the Rainbow* took off, too, and flew away with Sterling and Sparkle.

I have to admit, watching them go made me feel **SICK** to my stomach. I hoped the trolls weren't following us. Now that our group had split up, we were **WEAKER** and more **DEFENSELESS**. I was so nervous my left eye had begun to **twitch** and my paws were **shaking**.

How embarrassing!

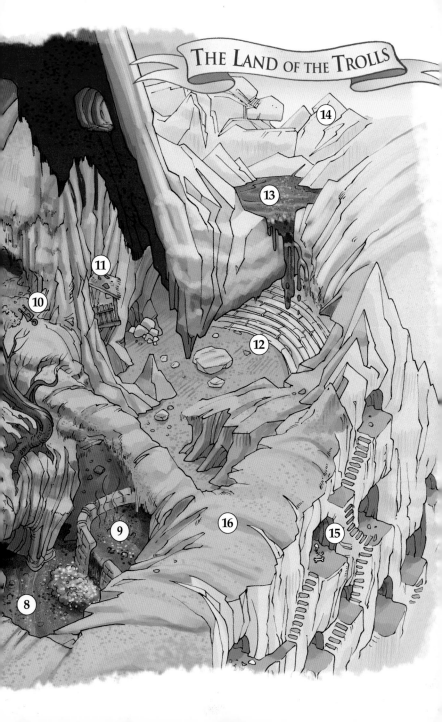

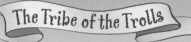

The Tribe of the Trolls

1. HALL OF FLEA AND SCAB-PICKING
2. HALL OF SNORES
3. HALL OF DRUM-DE-DRUM-DRUMMING
4. HALL OF THE TROLLIC THRONE
5. SHORTCUT TO THE KINGDOM OF THE WITCHES

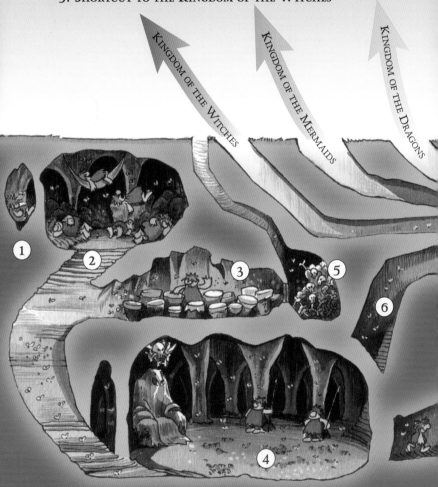

KINGDOM OF THE WITCHES

KINGDOM OF THE MERMAIDS

KINGDOM OF THE DRAGONS

6. Secret Passage to the Hall of the Trollic Throne
7. Exits to the Seven Kingdoms of Fantasy
8. Hall of Slop
9. Kitchen of Humongous Pots
10. Cupboard Filled with Rotten Meat
11. Sauna (the vapors rise from the kitchen)
12. Mud Shower Aromatized with Dragon's Dung
13. Dragon's Dung Depository

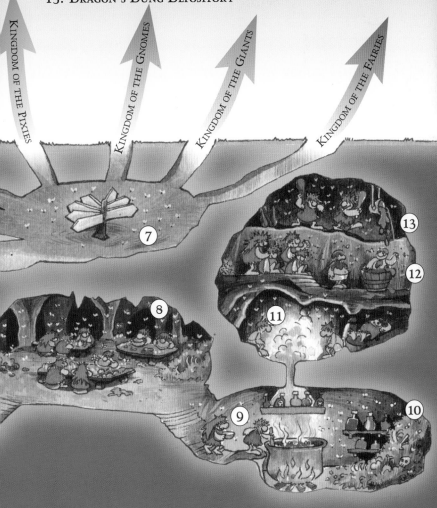

Kingdom of the Pixies

Kingdom of the Gnomes

Kingdom of the Giants

Kingdom of the Fairies

We trudged carefully through the Kingdom of the Trolls, trying to avoid the prickly bushes, rotten heads of cabbage, leftover bones, and **spoiled** food strewn everywhere. How **gross**!

Unfortunately, the Brand of Light was still **glowing** blue, so I knew we were still in grave danger. I was a furry bundle of nerves. Any minute I expected to hear the drum-de-drum-drum of the troll drums or see their ugly faces **popping** up from behind some heap, arrows drawn.

To keep calm, Scribblehopper began to recite a poem and Bitsy began to sing softly.

I was about to try whistling a happy tune to cheer myself up when suddenly I remembered ARCTICA, the nymph of snow, and her gift. It wasn't a gift that I could touch, but at that moment I knew it could save our lives. It was the gift of silence!

"**Ssssshhh!**" I warned the others. "If

the trolls hear us, we're **dead**!"

We continued along in a TENSE silence. It was so dark I could barely see my paw in front of my snout. We were trying not to follow the main paths, so the going was slow.

By the time we reached a cavern, it was already evening. A SIGN hung over the entrance. It was written in the Fantasian Alphabet. Can you translate it?*

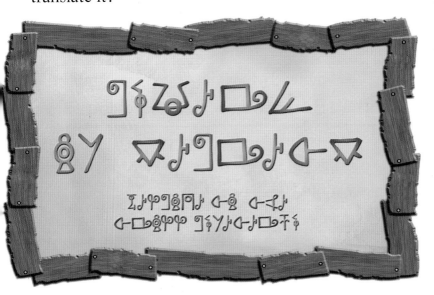

* You can find the Fantasian Alphabet on page 311.

The sign was hanging by one rusted nail, and the writing was **smudged** and hard to read. Yep, even their handwriting was **messy**!

I stuck my face as close to the sign as I could get without stepping on an old soup can and read the words out loud. It said **Cavern of Secrets**.

Secrets? I wondered what that meant. What kind of secrets could the trolls have? The secrets of being a **slob**? Of never bathing? Of steering clear of **deodorant**? Of picking your nose daily?

The more I thought about it, the more **disgusted** I became. Then I noticed something else written in very tiny letters under CAVERN OF SECRETS. But the writing was so **SMALL** I couldn't make it out.*

Oh well. There was no turning back now. We entered the cavern with hearts **thumping**.

* The very small writing on the sign says WELCOME TO THE TROLL CAFETERIA.

FIRST FROG
SOUP . . . THEN
STUFFED MOUSE!

As we entered the cave, the Brand of Light on my paw got **brighter**. Rancid rat hairs! That place must have been crawling with trolls.

My whiskers trembled with fear and my paws shook. I was dying to run screaming from the cave, but I couldn't. I knew the others were counting on me. Bitsy was hiding in my helmet. And Scribblehopper was croaking softly.

"Don't worry, Knight," the frog said. "If the trolls devour you, I'll write a **LONG**, wonderful poem about you. I won't even mention your shaky paws."

I rolled my eyes. I didn't want to tell him

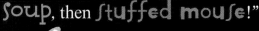
that if they ate me, they'd probably eat him.

Even though the cave was dark, I had the feeling that thousands of eyes were **spying** on us. It was **creepy**.

Then, without warning, we began to hear voices WHiSPERiNG in the darkness.

"Well, look at that! They fell for our trick. I was smart to make the letters so small!"

"If they didn't read the sign carefully, that's **TOO BAD** for them!"

"Should we grab them?"

"Let's EAT them as an appetizer!"

"I'm the boss. I say first **frog soup**, then **stuffed mouse**!"

Here's Bitsy!

YIKES!

Something told me that I should have done a better job of reading the sign at the entrance to the cave — especially the **fine** print!

A moment later, the trolls grabbed us, **shut** us into their enormouse dark pantry, and left.

FESTERING FRUITCAKE! We had walked right into the kitchen of the troll cafeteria!

From the **smell**, I could tell that the room was

Here's Bitsy!

filled with **stinky** troll food.

I walked over to the heavy wooden door of the pantry and peered through the keyhole.

There was a set of long tables full of jugs and chipped plates. In a corner was a big fireplace with a lit fire and an enormouse pot that **BoiLED** menacingly. Wooden spoons, huge forks, and pots of all sizes were hanging from the walls and dripping some kind of horrible **gReaSy LiQuiD**. . . .

Here's Bitsy!!

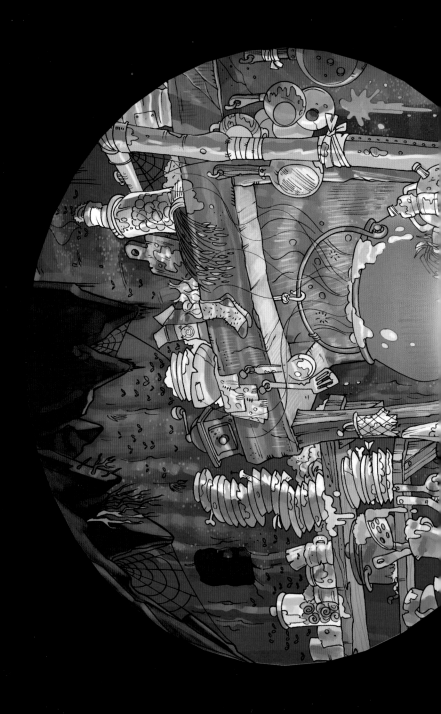

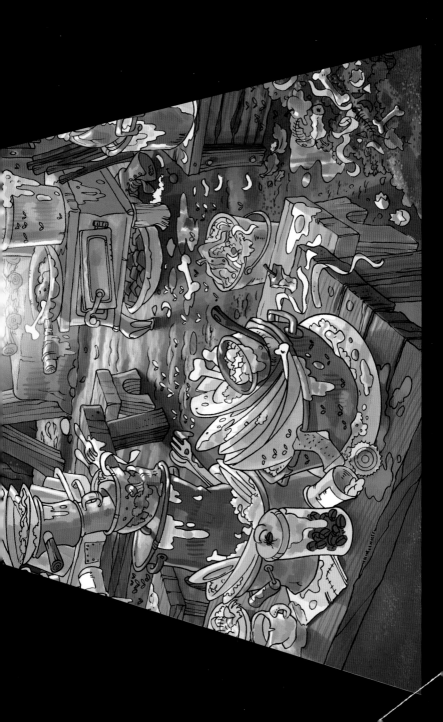

A Nice Giant Omelet!

As I was checking out the room, the trolls suddenly appeared. With them was a lady troll wearing a **dirty** chef's hat and carrying a **giant** pot in her hand.

"Okay, listen up, **Mixy**," said the biggest troll to the lady chef. "I want those pests cooked up nice and crispy. I want to be able to hear their little bones **crunch**. Too bad that annoying dragon lover **Sterling** didn't come with them. I always dreamed of having a princess at my table."

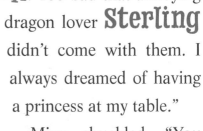

Mixy chuckled. "You mean **ON** your table, Chief Horrid," she said.

MIXY VON TROLL

NOSE PICKER

I couldn't believe those **ROTTEN** trolls.

For the next few minutes, the trolls went on and on about their next meal . . . er, I mean, they went on and on about **US**!

The other troll complained that there wouldn't be enough to eat. "The rodent is nice and **chubby**, but the frog is super-SKINNY," he whined.

CHIEF HORRID

Me, **chubby**? I was so insulted I wanted to burst out of the pantry screaming, "Who are you calling **chubby**?!"

I mean, don't get me wrong. I knew I had put on a few extra pounds recently. But it was all my cousin Brownie Whiskers's fault.

She had opened up a new bakery and had been sending me tons of samples. YUM!

I was dreaming about MINI-CHEESECAKES when a troll's voice broke into my thoughts.

"I have an idea. What if we make a nice GIANT omelet? Maybe we could even use the dragon egg," the troll suggested.

At this the leader of the trolls jumped up.

"No! No one TOUCHES the egg! Everyone gave their word as a TROLL!" he reminded them.

"Exactly, boss," another troll *snickered*. "Everyone knows how little a troll's word is worth! Too bad for that great big fool Firebreath. What a DUNCE to trust a troll!"

They laughed together.

"Hee hee hee...

hee hee hee"

Finally, they linked their grubby arms and **sang** this song:

"We are rude and very smelly!
We have giant big old bellies!
We like to crush and chew on bones!
Don't call us up —
We have no phones!
We live in caves —
they're dark and creepy.
But we're not scared,
and never weepy!
Our teeth are rotten,
and beware —
a fight with a troll is
never fair!"

BA-BUM . . .
BA-BUM . . .
BA-BUM . . .

I was fuming.

So it really was true! Firebreath III was a big old **liar** and a big old TRAITOR. Why had he done it?

I had no idea. But I had no time to figure it out, either. There were two MORE-URGENT problems I needed to solve:

(1) How not to become the daily special, and

(2) how to save the dragon egg!

Hmmm . . . the dragon egg. That got me thinking. The trolls had spoken about making an omelet. Maybe the dragon egg was hidden in the DARK pantry with us!

I did my best to check out every corner of the pantry. Too bad all I could find was pile after pile of **disgusting** troll food, like . . .

- **7** barrels of SOUR LEMON RINDS
- **4** rounds of **wandering cheese**
(The cheese moves by itself because of all the worms!)
- **2** jars of **stinky-sock** extract
- **12** tubes of super-concentrated **mold**
- **81** cans of candied black ooze, *onion* flavored
- **15** buckets of slimy SLUG JUICE
- **5** jars of chopped TOENAILS

YUCK!

The troll food was so **gross** I almost fainted. What kind of **crazy** lunatic would want to eat toenails and drink slug juice? Even if I were starving to death, I would **never** try

those things. Well, maybe I could try the *sour* lemon rinds. I did love these *sour* lemon candies my nephew had one Halloween. . . .

I was remembering those lemon candies when I spied something strange. Tucked in one dark corner, an enormouse cloth sack was sitting on a pile of hay.

WHAT WAS INSIDE????

Slowly, I opened the sack.

Cheese niblets!

It was the **dragon egg**!

It was speckled with **PINK** and **BLUE** splotches, and **shined** softly in the darkness. When I reached out to touch it, I felt something moving inside. **Holey cheese!**

There was something alive and growing inside that egg and I knew exactly what it was! It was a **BABY DRAGON**!

I was so excited I almost let out a loud **squeak** by accident. Luckily, I remembered the **TROLLS** waiting to eat us just outside the door. Instead, I put my ear up to the egg's shell and listened happily to the steady heartbeat inside:

ba-bum ba-bum ba-bum ba-bum . . .
ba-bum ba-bum ba-bum ba-bum . . .
ba-bum ba-bum ba-bum ba-bum . . .
ba-bum ba-bum ba-bum ba-bum . . .

It sounds weird, but at that moment I felt a special bond with the egg. Well, not with the egg itself but with the baby **GROWING** inside. After all, the baby dragon was **DEFENSELESS**

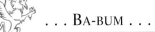
and needed our help. I **VOWED** I would do my best to protect it.

"Don't worry," I whispered to the egg. "We'll save you!"

TAKE THIS!

A moment later, Bitsy flew over and landed on my helmet.

"Knight, I've been thinking, this **TROLL** thing isn't looking so good. They're getting ready to **FRY** you up. Maybe now would be a good time for me to fly off and go ask for help. I can find Sterling and guide her here with the rest of the Silver Dragons," she suggested.

I hated to see Bitsy go, but I knew she was right.

It would be hard enough to *escape* from the trolls without the egg. But now we'd have to figure out a way to bring it with us.

"Good luck!" I whispered to Bitsy as she slid through the **keyhole** and flew off in search of help.

With a **SINKING** heart I watched Bitsy fly

away. Who knew if we would ever see the little ladybug again?

Still, there was no time to get weepy. Time was running out. We needed to come up with a way to escape. I had a bad feeling that the cook was getting ready to turn us into **frog soup**, **STUFFED MOUSE**, and **DRAGON OMELET**!

Unfortunately, no ideas were coming to mind.
NO IDEAS.
NO IDEAS.
NO IDEAS.

In fact, the more I thought, the less I came up with. **Rats!** I was so scared, my brain had turned to mush!

Distractedly, I slipped my paw into my bag to look for something that could be **USEFUL**. I pulled out the rosebud. Now what could I do with that?

I stared at the flower, feeling desperate. Oh, how I wished I were home in my **COZY MOUSE HOLE**!

Then the door burst open.

It was Mixy, the troll cook!

Without thinking, I held up my paw that was holding the rose toward Mixy and squeaked, **"TAKE THIS!"**

Then I closed my eyes, expecting to feel Mixy's rolling pin **BASHING** me over the head at any second. . . .

But **NOTHING** happened. The blow never came.

I couldn't believe it. What was Mixy **waiting** for?

After a while, I opened my **EYES**.

The lady troll stood with the rolling pin hanging by her side and tears in her eyes.

"No one has ever given me a *ROSE* before," she said. And with that, she began to **bawl** her eyes out.

WHAT CAN I MAKE FOR DINNER?

At first I wasn't sure what to do. Was Mixy losing her marbles? Who gets that emotional over a *flower*? Then it hit me. The *rosebud* had been given to me out of kindness. And now I had given it to Mixy. She had never been treated *kindly* before.

Suddenly, I knew what I had to do. I grabbed the troll's filthy hand and said, "This is for you, *dear lady.*"

Oh, thank you!

It's for you!

She **bluЅhed** and began to cry again. "Oh, thank you, Knight. No one ever treated me so kindly before," she **sobbed**. "But now what am I going to do? Those guys are STARVING out there, and I don't want to **cook** you after you were so nice to me. Oh, this is a nightmare! What can I make for dinner?"

Scribblehopper HOPPED over. "I have an idea. How about tonight *we* cook!?" he croaked.

THE SECRET
INGREDIENT!

Mixy led us to the kitchen. "Okay, here is the pot, and here are the ingredients. But there'll be **TROUBLE** if the trolls find out that you guys aren't **IN** the soup, too!" she warned.

Then she took off her apron and left happily, smelling the *rose*, while we began to prepare the dinner.

Here are the things we put into the **SOUP**: rotten **FISH**, fermented potato sprouts, boiled larvae, super-concentrated **STINKY** cabbage, curdled milk, **sour** cream, dishwater, **toenail** dirt, ogre earwax, troll dandruff, a spoonful of fresh cockroaches, and, finally, a secret ingredient that made the cauldron stink terribly!

Here is the Trolls' SOUP!
Made by
Geronimo and Scribblehopper

EVEN GROSSER THAN CURDLED MILK . . .

. . . EVEN VILER THAN BOILED LARVAE . . .

. . . THE MYSTERIOUS INGREDIENT IS . . . STINKY TROLL SOCKS!

We put the **smelly** soup on the fire and returned to the pantry to protect the **dragon egg** and wait for the trolls. We got there just in time.

A minute later, the **STARVING** trolls began to arrive. They stormed **NOISILY** into the cave and threw themselves down onto the benches surrounding a long table.

Then Chief Horrid, leader of the trolls, **punched** the table.

"Mixy! Where are you? I'm **HUNGRY**! Where is my **frog soup**? Where is my **STUFFED MOUSE**?" he demanded.

Mixy grabbed the soup and *twirled* into the room. I noticed she had brushed her hair and tucked the rose behind her ear.

The chief scowled at her. "What's with the *ROSE*?" he growled. Then he saw the pot. "Mmm . . . now that smells good. Very **stinky**," he remarked. "Now get lost. And lose the rosebud. It looks ridiculous."

Sadly, Mixy slunk from the room.

RATS! MORE CLIMBING!

Mixy returned to the pantry in tears.

"Do you see how they treat me? Like I'm some kind of dumb servant with no feelings! I'm sick of it! I don't ever want to cook for those guys again!" she sobbed.

I put my paw on Mixy's **HUGE** hand. She was right. No one should be treated so badly. "Don't worry, Mixy. If we ever get out of this place, you can come with us! But first we need to get out of here fast, and take the egg with us!"

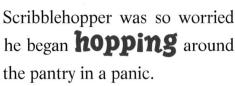

Scribblehopper was so worried he began **hopping** around the pantry in a panic.

"They're going to eat us!" he cried.

In his panic, he tripped over my bag, spilling out the golden seeds.

And the seeds began SPROUTING.

What an incredible gift!

In a few seconds, the seeds grew

and grew and grew until they touched the ceiling.

The branches became *thick* and strong, moving toward the sky, trying to find the light!

With a crack, they CRUSHED the rocks on the roof of the cave and opened up a gap of sky. We were FREE!

Well, almost free. First we had to **climb** up the branches while carrying the egg. **Rats!** More climbing!

Plus, we needed to move **FAST.** Any minute the trolls would be after us. I was so stressed I twisted my tail into a knot. **Ouch!** If only we had more **time** . . .

Then I remembered the GOLDEN HOURGLASS. I pulled it out and pressed the button, and the sand stopped.

Hooray! We now had one whole extra hour!

THE GREAT DRAGON BATTLE

No, More to the Left . . .

We started climbing up the trunk of the strange **giant** plant.

The climb was hard and **dangerous** and seemed like it would take forever. Every few minutes, the plant **shook** uncontrollably and I felt like I would **splatter** to the ground. Even worse, I was holding the enormouse **dragon egg**, and I couldn't see a thing! I felt like one of the three **BLIND** mice dressed up as a knight.

Scribblehopper guided me from above while Mixy brought up the rear.

Up and up and up we climbed. . . .

I did my best not to think about falling, **DROPPING** the egg, letting down my friends, not completing our **mission**, disappointing Sterling, or being eaten by the **FEROCIOUS** trolls.

But the more I thought about *not* thinking about those things, the more I thought about them! My paws began shaking, rattling the egg.

Scribblehopper tried to help. "Don't worry, Knight! You're almost to the top. Just listen to my instructions and you'll be fine. Now, put your **RiGHt** foot more to the **LeFt** and your **LeFt** paw more to the **RiGHt**, then move your **RiGHt** paw more to the **RiGHt** and move your **RiGHt** foot more to the **RiGHt**, no, more to the **LEFT**— no, I mean **RIGHT**. I mean to *my* **RIGHT** . . . which is your **LEFT**. Or is that my **LEFT**? Oops, Knight, which one is *my* **LEFT** again?"

Even though part of me wanted to strangle Scribblehopper, I was concentrating so hard, trying to understand his ridiculous directions and **climb** one foot at a time . . . that I actually forgot to be afraid!

Soon we reached the top of a **ROCKY HiLL**. We had done it! We were **FREE**!

Exhausted, I placed the egg on a soft bit of **moss**.

> **CONQUERING FEAR**
> One secret to conquering your fear is to stay calm and determined and move at your own pace. The more you try, the better you will feel about yourself!

"Good thing you tripped on my bag and those seeds sprouted. Otherwise, we'd probably be **troll soup** by now!" I told Scribblehopper.

He grinned. "Oh, it wasn't hard, Knight," he said. "I just started hopping around like this and . . ." BANG!

Scribblehopper tripped again!

"**Watch the egg!**" I squeaked.

But it was too late. The egg began to roll down the mountain!

Without thinking, I raced after it, grabbed it, and began rolling down along with it all the way to the valley. Scribblehopper and Mixy RAN after me.

Right then, the trolls' drums began to sound. They had discovered our escape!

DID SOMEONE
CALL ME?

I was looking around frantically for somewhere to **HIDE** when, suddenly, Sparkle, Sterling, and Bitsy landed in front of us.

They were a sight for **SORE** eyes! We were all so excited to see one another we hugged happily. For a moment, I almost forgot about the **TROLLS**.

"How was your trip?" I asked Bitsy.

"Not bad," the ladybug replied. "I not only found Sterling, the Silver Dragons, *and* the *Dragon of the Rainbow,* but I also met a friendly ant who led me to Elf Woods. I found **THUNDERHORN**, King of the Elves, who promised he would lead his troops here."

Right at that moment we heard a **deep** voice announce, "Did someone call me? I, **THUNDERHORN**, have arrived!"

We turned to see a majestic white deer trotting up.

"WELCOME TO THE COMPANY, KING THUNDERHORN!" EVERYONE CHEERED.

A feeling of relief **washed** over me. King Thunderhorn was confident and **COURAGEOUS.**

He had been a big help in my previous battles in the Kingdom of Fantasy. I knew he could help us this time, too.

"Never fear!" the deer proclaimed. "My

Thunderhorn

King Thunderhorn is the mysterious King of the Forest Elves. No one knows why he always appears as a white deer, though there are rumors that Cackle caused it. Thunderhorn is wise, courageous, and always ready to defend those in trouble. He has snowy white fur, and his horns are made of pure gold.

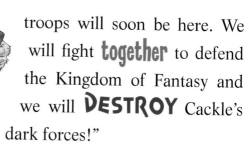

troops will soon be here. We will fight **together** to defend the Kingdom of Fantasy and we will **DESTROY** Cackle's dark forces!"

See what I mean about **confidence**? That deer had a ton of it!

Just then Mixy spoke up. "Um, excuse me, everyone," she said, **waving** her rolling pin in the air. "But would it be okay if I joined in the fight?"

After introducing Mixy, I cheered along with everyone:

"WELCOME TO THE COMPANY, MIXY VON TROLL!"

THE BATTLE!

It was already nightfall when I saw two threatening CLOUDS on the horizon.

Then I took a better look. They weren't clouds after all. They were two armies that were approaching each other.

From the east came the SILVER DRAGONS and King Thunderhorn's army of elves. From the west came Cackle's dark forces. These included the DRAGONS OF FIRE with King Firebreath III at the command, the HEARTLESS KNIGHTS — empty armor guided by Cackle's wickedness — the TERRIFYING TROLLS, and a group of enormouse and CRUEL OGRES. The EVIL forces outnumbered us by far.

I gulped. I had a feeling this wasn't going to be a very fair fight.

Instinctively, we gathered around the **egg** to protect it. Sterling prepared her bow, Thunderhorn lowered his head to assume the **ATTACK** position, Mixy waved her rolling pin, and Scribblehopper and I? Well, since we didn't have any **weapons**, we hung on to the **egg**, ready to shield it from an attack.

Then I spotted Cackle on her Black Dragon. Her icy-cold laugh thundered in the night.

HA! HA! HA! HA! HA! HA!

"Knight, I challenge you! We have a score to settle, you and me! Now you will taste the fire of my **Black Dragon**!" she shrieked.

THE BLACK DRAGON?

How strange. I remembered that a long time before, I had hit him in a duel with my **RING OF LIGHT**. I scratched my head. "B-but didn't he leave town a long time ago?" I asked.

"Yes, you **dirty rat**! You ruined my old dragon. He's not into **EVIL** things anymore. This is his **twin brother**. But enough about dragons. Now I will make you pay! I will **destroy** the kingdom of your friend Sterling, then I will take over all of the **KINGDOM OF FANTASY!**"

What could I do? I had to accept the challenge.

I summoned the *Dragon of the Rainbow*. Then, trying to look courageous, I took a running leap to get up onto his back. Unfortunately, I missed. After a few more running starts and a few more misses, the **DRAGON** gave me a boost.

"Ready, Knight?" Cackle scoffed.

Before I could answer, I heard a thunderlike **boom** and felt the ground begin to **shake**. A thousand dragons took flight into the sky.

THE BATTLE HAD BEGUN!

I was immediately attacked by Cackle's Black Dragon, who blew a dangerous **FIREBALL** in my direction. The Dragon of the Rainbow pulled away quickly, but still my whiskers got **singed**. Youch!

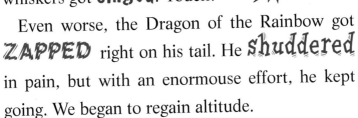

Even worse, the Dragon of the Rainbow got **ZAPPED** right on his tail. He **shuddered** in pain, but with an enormouse effort, he kept going. We began to regain altitude.

We flew **higher and higher and higher**. In fact, we were flying so high I was getting short of breath. I needed **OXYGEN**!

My charred whiskers became covered with ice.

But then they suddenly felt better — the dragon had flown higher so that the **frosty air** would soothe our burnt body parts.

But the Dragon of the Rainbow was too weak to fly that **HIGH** for long. He lost control and we began to **fall**.

My life **flashed** before my eyes: *My first squeak. My first nibble of cheese.* Then, luckily, the **leaves** on the trees broke our fall.

Then Cackle **SPOTTED** me. She lifted her pinky and shot a tremendous **lightning bolt** my way. It was headed right toward me, but Thunderhorn THREW himself in front of me to protect me . . . and saved my life!

I stared in sorrow at the **huge deer** on the ground. His breathing was shallow and his eyes were half-shut. "It was a worthy battle . . . ," he whispered.

I was CRUSHED. My friend was dying before my eyes. I had to do something! But what?

Then I remembered the **SPECIAL** vial of water in my bag. The nymph had said, *"Just one drop can heal wounds, one sip gives strength, and two sips bring youth."*

Quickly, I tried to pour **one drop** into Thunderhorn's mouth. But Cackle arrived, and my paws began to shake. MORE THAN TWO DROPS fell into

Thunderhorn's lips. Oh, no!

There was a *flash of light*. . . .

Suddenly, instead of a white deer with golden horns, a young elf prince stood before me.

"Thank you, Knight!" he said. "You have broken Cackle's spell!"

I have to admit I had not expected my **DEER** friend suddenly to become an **elf prince**! But either way, I was glad he was alive.

In fact, I was so happy that **THUNDERHORN** was okay that I almost forgot about Cackle.

When I turned back, I saw her mounting her **Black Dragon**.

"You've won for now, Rodent Knight!" she shrieked. "Once you've reversed one of my spells, I'm powerless for **twenty-four** hours. But I'm not done with you!"

She flew off in a **rage**.

Tap Tap Tap

Now that the **WITCH** had left with her dark forces, there were only the **DRAGONS** left on the battlefield. Still, things were pretty ugly between the **DRAGONS OF FIRE** and the **Silver Dragons**. Neither side was willing to call it quits.

I was trying to decide what to do next when I heard a strange sound.

TAP TAP TAP!

It was the **dragon egg**!

With a crack, it split open, and a **little boy dragon** and a **little girl dragon** emerged!

Their bodies were covered with scales

that shined like DIAMONDS. They looked at me with curious eyes, then they staggered over to me and rubbed their snouts in my fur.

What could I do? I HUGGED them to me. Poor little guys. They had really picked the wrong time to hatch. Right in the middle of a battle!

I felt terrible. I had to do something to stop this crazy fighting. In desperation, I dug through my bag, looking for something — anything — that might help. I pulled out the olive branch, a symbol of peace.

Right then, I knew what I needed to do. I had to stop that useless battle!

It was almost dawn, but the sky was DARK. The battling DRAGONS had taken a rest and all was quiet. It reminded

BUILDING PEACE

A world without wars and conflicts is hard to imagine, but each one of us can do our part to make peace happen. You can do this by respecting others and trying to discuss any problems fairly.

me of something my old history teacher once talked about — "the calm before the storm."

The **battle** was about to start again.

I took advantage of the silence and yelled as loudly as I could, "**STOP**, everyone! The egg has **HATCHED**!

"IT'S USELESS TO KEEP FIGHTING!"

No one answered. Uh-oh. *Now you've done it, Geronimo*, I thought. Why hadn't I just run away? I should have known no one would listen to a **MOUSE** dressed up in a **KNIGHT** costume.

I closed my eyes and hugged the two **baby** dragons.

OH, WHAT A TRAGEDY!

But then, all of a sudden, I began to hear the **DRAGONS** murmuring. It started low at first; then their voices grew louder.

"He's right!"

"Why are we fighting?"

"The **egg has hatched** already!"

"Yeah, what's the point?"

"This is ridiculous!"

Firebreath III stood in the middle of the battlefield, furious. "What is the matter with you?" he screamed at his army of dragons. "Attack them! What are you waiting for? Cackle promised me that once Sterling was out of the picture, I'd be **king** of all the dragons! Now ATTACK! ATTACK! ATTACK!"

But no one moved.

Finally, Sterling approached through the crowd. She spoke in a STRONG, clear voice. "Valiant DRAGONS OF FIRE, we are all brothers here. Stop fighting! These two **baby** dragons have found their trainer. It is he, the Twelfth Knight. There will be no more war between us now. Only PEACE!"

As soon as Sterling finished speaking, a ray of sun hit the scales on the two baby dragons' backs,

creating a fabumouse **Rainbow**.

Then all the dragons cheered together, "**LONG LIVE THE TWELFTH KNIGHT!**"

Normally, I would have been embarrassed by all the attention, but I was so **happy** I took a bow.

LONG LIVE PEACE!

I Was Jealous

While everyone was cheering, Firebreath III tried to slip away. But Mixy von Troll was on him like my uncle Cheesebelly on a plate of donuts.

"Where do you think you're going, wise guy?" she yelled.

Sterling ordered her dragons PING and PONG to seize him. They caught him in a second, dragging him KICKING AND SCREAMING by his tail. Then Sterling played her silver flute and the other members of the Great Dragon Council gathered around.

"Firebreath III, you have BETRAYED the dragon race, you have aligned yourself with the wicked Cackle, you didn't hesitate to put the lives of the baby dragons at risk, and you tried to taint my HONOR and get me thrown out of the kingdom. **WHY** did you do it?" the princess demanded.

Firebreath hung his head. "I was jealous of you, Princess," he admitted with a sniffle. "I was jealous of your kingdom. I was jealous of your good relationship with Blossom. So one night when Cackle came and proposed that I **STEAL** the egg and make it look like your fault, I accepted. I told her everything — the hiding place, and the SeCReT PASSWORD. Then I *stole* the egg and I gave it to the trolls to look after. I am so sorry. It was wrong to **BETRAY** you. It was wrong to trust the **wicked witch**," he sobbed.

Right at that moment, **Blossom**, the Queen

JEALOUSY

Jealousy makes us feel angry and hostile toward others. When we are jealous, we often feel bad about ourselves. If you feel jealous, try not to compare yourself to others. Remember everyone is different, and everyone is special!

of the Fairies, and George, the King of Dreams, arrived riding a white unicorn. Everyone bowed respectfully as they approached.

When they arrived at the center of the clearing, George said, "We are thrilled that good and peace and justice have triumphed!"

Meanwhile, Blossom turned to me. "Knight, once again you have brought harmony to the Kingdom of Fantasy. How can we repay you?" she asked. "Would you like your own unicorn, a GOLD watch, or maybe tickets to the new FAIRY OPERA? I haven't been, but I hear it's delightful!"

I smiled. It would be fun to have my own unicorn. Imagine what my coworkers at *The Rodent's Gazette* would say! But in the end, I told the queen that I didn't want anything. She was such a kind person. And I really was just happy to help the Kingdom of Fantasy!

Finally, Blossom addressed FIREBREATH.

"Firebreath, you let jealousy, envy, and the thirst for power **POISON** your heart. You believed in Cackle's lies. I'm afraid we have no choice but to apply the Dragon Law and **BANISH** you far, far away from your kingdom," she said.

Firebreath stared at the ground, looking **MISERABLE**. I felt bad for him.

So I dared to interrupt.

"Umm, excuse me, Queen Blossom. I know I said I didn't want **ANYTHING**, but actually, there is something that I would like to ask for, if it's not too late . . . ," I began.

Everyone stared at me, stunned.

They probably were thinking I had reconsidered the watch offer, but this was way more **important** than a piece of jewelry. What I wanted to ask for was a **SECOND CHANCE** for Firebreath.

"I know Firebreath messed up, but I think he understands his **mistake**. Everyone can **CHANGE** if they're given a chance!" I said. "I think he can improve himself."

The queen smiled. "Knight, your heart is **large**. And so it shall be! Now place your left paw on Firebreath's **heart**!" she ordered.

I **flinched**. I have to admit that even though I was feeling kindly toward Firebreath, he still scared me a little. But I did as I was told. And when my trembling paw touched his scale-covered chest, the Brand of Light gave off a *blue light* that touched Firebreath's body like an electric shock. Then he opened his eyes wide. I was surprised to see they no longer looked angry.

Firebreath sighed. "Wow! I feel so happy and good! I know I made a mess of things, Queen Blossom. I would really like to try to make it up to all of the DRAGONS. But how?" he said.

THANK YOU!

Just then, the two **DRAGON** babies, who had been hiding behind me, **stumbled** toward Firebreath. They sniffed him curiously. Then they **hugged** his knees.

"They **like** me! They really **like** me!" he said, grinning from ear to ear.

Blossom beamed. "Did you see that? Now that his heart is **good**, even the babies noticed. That gives me an idea. If it's okay with you, Knight, perhaps Firebreath can take care of raising the little dragons to be **good** and **kind**. He will stay here in the Kingdom of the Silver Dragons and take care of them until they are old enough to be on their own.

"Then it will be up to you, Knight, to teach them **acrobatics**. Only you will be able to ride them," she said.

Teach them **acrobatics**? I was glad the dragons were only babies for now. I'd have to read up on that subject. Did I mention I'm not much of a sportsmouse?

I gave the babies one last **hug** and then they ran back to Firebreath.

"THANK you! THANK you! THANK you!" Firebreath exclaimed. "I promise I will take care of them as if they were my own children, and I will raise them according to the Dragon Law. We will be a real *family*!"

Blossom, George, and Sterling looked at one another, then nodded and said solemnly, "And so it shall be!"

At that moment I felt the palm of my paw

STING and I noticed that the Brand of Light had disappeared. For the first time since I had left, I felt HOMESICK.

"The **BRAND OF LIGHT** has vanished because you have completed your mission," Sterling explained. "You saved the **dragon egg** and my kingdom, you planted the seeds for lasting peace, and you turned a *bad* dragon into a **good** one."

All the dragons grunted:

"THANK YOU! THANK YOU!"

I must say I was feeling pretty proud of myself. This trip had been quite an adventure!

But now it was time to say good-bye.

I climbed back onto the *Dragon of the Rainbow* and we took off into the sky. Part of me felt sad about leaving, but somehow I knew this wouldn't be my last visit to the Kingdom of Fantasy.

As I waved to the baby dragons, who were ʃqueɑking and **squealing** good-bye, I thought I heard the happy sound of bells. . . .

Ding Dong Ding Dong Ding Dong
Ding Dong Ding Dong Ding Dong

THE RETURN TO
NEW MOUSE CITY

HOME, SWEET HOME!

Ding Dong Ding Dong Ding Dong
Ding Dong Ding Dong Ding Dong

The sound of the bells followed me home. I woke up, shocked to find myself in my cozy mouse bed. I smiled. Home, sweet home!

At that moment I heard the noise again:

Ding Dong Ding Dong Ding Dong
Ding Dong Ding Dong Ding Dong

I shook my head. Was something wrong with my ears? Then I realized it was the **doorbell**! I went down to see who was ringing it.

My nephew Benjamin stood on the stoop. "Hi, Uncle!" he squeaked. "You are a **HEAVY** sleeper. I've been ringing the **bell** for a whole hour!"

"I'm so sorry, Benjamin. I must have been *dreaming*," I said.

My nephew giggled and handed me my newspaper. "It's okay, Uncle, but you've got to hurry," he said. "Turn on the television. Check out the news!"

I switched on the TV and on the news I saw . . . myself! It was me at the grand opening of the DRAGON exhibit!

Then I noticed the newspaper headline. It was about the dragon exhibit, too. "A **sensational**

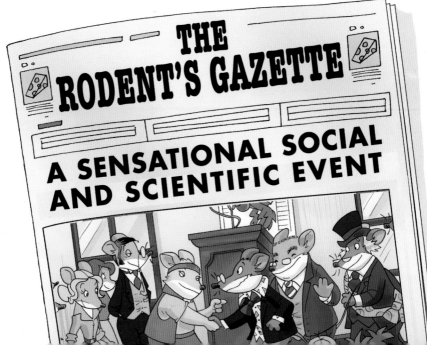

THE RODENT'S GAZETTE

A SENSATIONAL SOCIAL AND SCIENTIFIC EVENT

social and scientific event hosted by Geronimo Stilton!"

Back on television they were doing a *fashion* segment.

"Popular publisher and author Geronimo Stilton sets a new trend that's **spreading** like cream cheese! It's the pajama top! It's not just for sleeping anymore! Famouse journalist Sally

Ratmousen has already coined it 'THE FASHION TREND OF THE YEAR'!"

I was in shock. I clicked off the television and looked out the window.

It was unbelievable! Mice were RUSHING everywhere dressed in their PJ'S! Well, in their PJ TOPS, to be exact. Not bottoms. But still, they were running around in their pajamas just like I had done on the night of the grand opening! Who would have thought I, *Geronimo Stilton*, could have started a fashion trend?

Benjamin and I burst out laughing. Fashion fads can be so ridiculous!

"Oh! Uncle Geronimo!" Benjamin said. "Did you remember that you promised me you would take me to the soccer game? The SQUEAKERS are playing!"

I froze. I had been so busy with the DRAGON exhibit opening, I had totally forgotten!

I was trying to figure out what to do when suddenly I remembered two tickets that a sports writer at *The Rodent's Gazette* had given me. Perfect!

Benjamin was so excited he gave me a huge hug. Then we quickly went to get ready.

I changed into my **SQUEAKERS** jersey, my **SQUEAKERS** hat, and my **SQUEAKERS** scarf. Go, Cheddar Bay **SQUEAKERS**!

We had time before the game started, so we decided to walk through the park.

After strolling around, we sat under a *beautiful* oak tree, enjoying the *gorgeous* fall day. Before long, we were joined by Benjamin's friends who were playing ball at a field nearby. I was having such a *wonderful*

time with my nephew on my beloved Mouse Island that my adventure in the **KINGDOM OF FANTASY** seemed like a long-ago dream.

Just then, one of Benjamin's friends said, "Please tell us a story, Mr. Stilton!"

"Yeah, a story!" everyone yelled.

So I began to tell them about my dream. I told them about the lost **dragon egg** and about the strange gifts of the **SEVEN SISTERS**. I told them about the evil **TROLLS** and about the battle between the dragons. I even told them about following the **DRAGON POOP**. For some reason they thought that part was really **funny**. Ugh!

In fact, Benjamin's friends liked my story **SO MUCH** that they convinced me to write it all down.

So here it is — the **BOOK** you have just finished reading!

FANTASIAN ALPHABET

ABOUT THE AUTHOR

Born in New Mouse City, Mouse Island, **GERONIMO STILTON** is Rattus Emeritus of Mousomorphic Literature and of Neo-Ratonic Comparative Philosophy. For the past twenty years, he has been running *The Rodent's Gazette*, New Mouse City's most widely read daily newspaper.

Stilton was awarded the Ratitzer Prize for his scoops on *The Curse of the Cheese Pyramid* and *The Search for Sunken Treasure*. He has also received the Andersen 2000 Prize for Personality of the Year. One of his bestsellers won the 2002 eBook Award for world's best ratlings' electronic book. His works have been published all over the globe.

In his spare time, Mr. Stilton collects antique cheese rinds and plays golf. But what he most enjoys is telling stories to his nephew Benjamin.

Don't miss my first three adventures in the Kingdom of Fantasy!

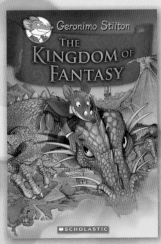

THE KINGDOM OF FANTASY

THE QUEST FOR PARADISE: THE RETURN TO THE KINGDOM OF FANTASY

THE AMAZING VOYAGE: THE THIRD ADVENTURE IN THE KINGDOM OF FANTASY

#19 My Name Is Stilton, Geronimo Stilton

#20 Surf's Up, Geronimo!

#21 The Wild, Wild West

#22 The Secret of Cacklefur Castle

A Christmas Tale

#23 Valentine's Day Disaster

#24 Field Trip to Niagara Falls

#25 The Search for Sunken Treasure

#26 The Mummy with No Name

#27 The Christmas Toy Factory

#28 Wedding Crasher

#29 Down and Out Down Under

#30 The Mouse Island Marathon

#31 The Mysterious Cheese Thief

Christmas Catastrophe

#32 Valley of the Giant Skeletons

#33 Geronimo and the Gold Medal Mystery

#34 Geronimo Stilton, Secret Agent

#35 A Very Merry Christmas

#36 Geronimo's Valentine

#37 The Race Across America

#38 A Fabumouse School Adventure

#39 Singing Sensation

#40 The Karate Mouse

#41 Mighty Mount Kilimanjaro

#42 The Peculiar Pumpkin Thief

#43 I'm Not a Supermouse!

#44 The Giant Diamond Robbery

#45 Save the White Whale!

#46 The Haunted Castle

#47 Run for the Hills, Geronimo!

#48 The Mystery in Venice

#49 The Way of the Samurai

#50 This Hotel is Haunted!

And coming soon!

#51 The Enormouse Pearl Heist